chapter
one

"**W**e've *got* to have a party this week," fourteen-year-old Chloe Carlson said to her twin sister Riley. "We have to make sure our social lives get off to an amazing start this year!"

"Totally," Riley agreed as they approached the steps of West Malibu High. She pulled her pageboy's cap off her head and shook out her shoulder-length blonde hair.

Chloe dropped her backpack on the steps so she could concentrate on the plan. "Can't you just picture it?" she went on. "The whole house will be decorated and fabulous. We'll have tons of great food and put lots of those scented candles all over the place. And we'll both get something new to wear, like—"

"I need to buy skinny black jeans," Riley interrupted, "to go with my sparkly blue sweater."

"Right," Chloe agreed, nodding and brushing her long wavy blonde hair over her shoulders. "And of course we'll have to find two totally great guys for dates."

"That's the whole point of the party, isn't it?" Riley grinned.

"Definitely!" Chloe glanced around, scanning the crowd of students hanging out, waiting for school to begin. She saw Stephen Briggs from algebra and Jason Green from her homeroom, but *the* guy, Travis Morgan — the one she most wanted to see — was nowhere in sight. Where is he? she wondered.

> [Chloe: Okay. So, you're reading this and you're wondering, Who's Travis Morgan? Travis Morgan just happens to be the cutest, the coolest, the number one guy on Chloe Carlson's top ten hotties at West Malibu High list. Scratch that. He's the ONLY one on the list! In other words. I totally have a crush on him.]

"Our house *is* perfect for it," Riley said, getting into the spirit of things. "I can see it now...an awesome party...walking on the beach afterwards...the moon overhead...and two guys..." She stopped. "But first we have to get Mom to say yes."

"Details," Chloe said with a shrug. "We'll talk to her after school today."

"Right," Riley said. Then she smiled. "So, are you going to do it? Are you going to ask Travis to the party?"

Chloe bit her lower lip, but gently — so she wouldn't mess up her lip gloss. "Don't rush me. I'm still working up the nerve just to *talk* to him. First I have to get past 'hi' before I ask him to a party."

"What party?" Rebecca Ravitz demanded, joining them. "Am I invited?"

"Yeah, what party?" Lauren Chambers chimed in.

Chloe hesitated for half a second. Did she really want to tell them? she wondered. Before she cleared the party with Mom?

And besides, Rebecca was the loudest girl in the ninth grade. She was funny and energetic, with blunt-cut red hair. Chloe liked the brightly coloured clothes Rebecca wore. The wild combinations fit her personality.

But she wasn't much good at keeping a secret. The word 'party' was already humming down the school steps and on to the lawn.

"What party?" Lauren repeated. Lauren was Rebecca's best friend. Her short, spiky black hair and pouty lips made her look like a model.

"We're thinking of having a thing on Friday night," Chloe explained. "And of course you'll be invited. I mean, everyone is. But – "

"Cool!" Rebecca said, whirling around to tell about a zillion people in the crowd nearby.

"Wait!" Chloe tried to stop her. But it was too late. Rebecca and Lauren were already spreading the word that there was a party at the Carlsons' on Friday night.

"Mistake," Riley said. "What if Mom says no to the party?"

"She *can't* say no," Chloe insisted. Then she checked her watch. The bell was about to ring. "We'd better go in. But wish me luck," she said, heading towards the door. "I'm going to try to run into Travis before or after third period. His locker is across the hall from Ms. Simmons's class."

"Okay, good luck," Riley said. "Not that you'll need it. I mean, if you don't catch him then, you can always talk to him at lunch, can't you?"

"No way," Chloe replied. "He hangs out at lunch with Kyle and Cameron."

"Ohhh," Riley said, nodding. "I guess it *would* be kind of hard to just walk up to *them* and start talking."

No kidding, Chloe thought. Kyle and Cameron were the coolest guys in the junior class. Travis was a junior, too, and when he was with his friends, he was totally unapproachable.

"Okay, so you'll find him after school," Riley added.

Chloe shook her head. "He has detention every day this week. The dirt bike thing, remember?"

Riley nodded again. Everyone in school knew about the dirt bike thing. Travis had somehow managed to get his bike into the building and ride it up and down the main hall. Chloe and her friends thought it was kind of funny – especially when Travis claimed that he needed the bike so he could get to class on time. But the vice principal, Mr. Conner, didn't agree.

"So, right around third period is, like, the only

chance you have to see him all day?" Riley asked her.

"Basically," Chloe replied.

"Wow," Riley said. "Talk about pressure."

"Tell me about it," Chloe said. "I get one or two chances a day to talk to him. And half the time, I blow it because I'm so nervous when I see him!"

The bell rang, and Chloe headed to homeroom. Later, paying attention in class was hopeless. She stared at the clock all through first and second periods, daydreaming.

Chloe pictured Travis walking along the beach — which is where she usually saw him. His short brown hair was lightened by the sun, making him look like a cute beach boy, even though he was more into riding his dirt bike on the sand than surfing the waves.

Finally the bell ending second period rang, and Chloe hurried to Ms. Simmons's room. She stood outside the door as she scoped out Travis's locker.

"Hi, Chloe!" Quinn Reyes called. She was one of Chloe's good friends, and one of the most social girls in the freshman class. "Do you want to practise for the junior varsity cheerleader try-outs with me? It's in a couple of weeks."

Chloe wasn't exactly sure if she wanted to be a cheerleader. But she didn't want to get caught up in a conversation with anybody in case Travis walked by. "Hey, can we talk about that later?" she asked. "I'm kind of waiting for you-know-who."

Quinn looked over her shoulder at Travis's locker and grinned. "Oh, riiiiiight. No problem. Catch you later!"

Chloe glanced at her watch. The third-period bell was going to ring any second. Where is he? she wondered, checking her watch. I hope he's not out sick.

"You coming?" Tara Jordan, another one of Chloe's friends called. She brushed past Chloe and headed into Ms. Simmons's room. "The bell's going to ring."

He's a no-show, Chloe thought. "Yeah, I'm coming," she answered. Her shoulders slumped as she walked into class and took her seat.

The bell rang. Chloe stared out the door at Travis's locker while Ms. Simmons wrote the next two history assignments on the board.

"All right, you know what the reading assignment is," Ms. Simmons began. "Now we're going to be doing a research project for the next two weeks. And I want you to work in pairs for this. I'm going to assign you each a partner."

Partners? Chloe's heart skipped a beat when she heard the word. That was what she wanted for her party on Friday – a partner. A partner named Travis Morgan. If only he weren't so hard to run into.

Almost as if her wish had come true, Travis suddenly appeared in Chloe's line of sight. He raced up to his locker in the hallway and dialled the combination quickly.

Late again, Chloe thought with a smile. Typical.

While Ms. Simmons paired off people in the class, Chloe watched him through the door window. She loved the shirt he was wearing. It was just a T-shirt, but the colour was awesome. A really deep turquoise blue.

"Justin and Annabelle," Ms. Simmons said, pairing up students. "Marco and Brittany...Dylan and Tara..."

Chloe and Travis, Chloe thought, adding her own pair to the list Ms. Simmons was calling out. She doodled 'Chloe 'n' Travis' on a clean page in her notebook and drew cute little hearts all around it. Then she closed her eyes and tried to imagine what it would be like to kiss Travis – the boy of her dreams.

[**Chloe:** **Come on. Don't tell me you've never done this. Everybody has.**]

"Chloe and Amanda," Ms. Simmons announced from the front of the room.

"Huh?" Chloe blurted out, snapping back to reality.

"I said, you and Amanda will be partners," Ms. Simmons repeated, frowning a little.

"Oh. Thanks." Chloe blushed slightly. She glanced at Amanda Grey to check her out. Amanda was about the quietest girl in school. She had moved to Malibu from San Francisco more than a year ago, but she was so shy, she still hadn't managed to fit in with any group of friends.

Chloe usually sat at the same lunch table as Amanda, since all of Chloe's friends ate lunch during different periods. But Chloe and Amanda never talked much to each other.

She's really very pretty, Chloe said to herself. Her long brown hair is thick and really shiny. And she has a perfectly shaped face. If she pulled back her hair, everyone would see how pretty she is. And if she wore a little make-up, she'd be more than pretty – she'd be *gorgeous*.

It might be fun to do a makeover on her, Chloe thought as she doodled a picture of Amanda with Cleopatra eyes. She glanced at the girl's high-waisted jeans and tucked-in shirt. And I could probably give her a few fashion tips to update her look a little, Chloe decided.

Then Ms. Simmons started explaining the research project, and Chloe actually had to pay attention.

For the next thirty minutes, she tried to concentrate on history. But her doodling hand kept writing the words 'party' and 'Travis' and 'moonlight stroll' all over the margins of her notebook page.

Finally the bell rang. She jumped out of her seat, hoping to catch Travis at his locker between classes. Her heart started pounding the minute she even *thought* about trying to talk to him.

She pushed her way through the doorway and then waited.

Was he coming? Maybe he didn't need to get his books this period. Or put anything away.

Then she saw him. Strolling down the middle of the

hall, as if he owned the place. He made a quick cut to the left, towards his locker.

Now's my chance, Chloe thought. Taking a deep breath, she put on her best smile and started to walk towards him. Almost there, she thought. Only a few feet away...

Suddenly her right foot slipped in her platform flip-flop. "Aaaarguhh!" she cried as she stumbled into a row of lockers – right next to Travis.

Travis stared at her. "You okay?"

She gazed into his deep brown eyes and felt herself turning bright red. "Heh-heh...um, so...um, what's shakin', uh, I mean, um, what's going on? What's – "

[Chloe: Somebody stop me. Please. Stop me now!]

"Maybe I should ask *you* that question," Travis said with a laugh.

Chloe's blush burned brighter. I knew I should have stuck with single syllables! She let out an involuntary giggle as she tried to think of something else to say. "Uh, I was just, um..."

Before she could finish her sentence – or even come up with one – someone tapped her on the shoulder. She turned and saw Mr. Conner, the vice principal, standing in the hall behind her.

"Miss Carlson, I'm glad I found you," Mr. Conner said. "I have some wonderful news. Since you've been so helpful with the Malibu High beautification project and you continue to tutor some students in algebra, you've been named West Malibu High's Good Citizen of the Month for the second time in a row."

"Oh." Chloe tried to smile even though she wasn't thrilled with the news. "Thanks a lot, Mr. Conner."

[Chloe: Who could blame me, right? I mean, Good Citizen isn't exactly the coolest award ever. But I can't help it if I'm responsible and like to help out my fellow freshmen!]

"Come to my office before lunch, and I'll give you the certificate," Mr. Conner said.

"Sure," Chloe told him. Then she turned back to Travis. She decided to be positive. Maybe Travis would actually think winning Good Citizen was a really great accomplishment...

"See ya, citizen," Travis said with a smirk. He closed his locker and headed off.

...Or not, Chloe thought with a sigh.

How could she ever ask him to her party after this?

chapter two

"**I** am *so* depressed," Chloe announced as she caught up with her sister in the hall a few minutes later.

"What's wrong?" Riley asked. "Another girl with the same shoes?"

"Worse," Chloe said. She held up the certificate the vice principal had given her. "I'm Good Citizen of the Month – again! And Travis heard Mr. Conner give me the news."

Riley shrugged. "Am I missing something here?" she asked. "What's the problem?"

Chloe rolled her eyes. "Riley, this certificate represents promptness, class participation, and good work habits. If I keep this up, I'm going to get a reputation!"

"Oh, yeah, I can see it now," Riley joked. "Written on the wall in the boys' locker room: For a good example, call Chloe."

"Ha ha." Chloe moaned. "Look – you have a free period

now. Come eat with me. I need some moral support."

"Okay," Riley agreed. "I don't have to study for a test. Besides, we can talk about the party, too."

They headed down to the cafeteria, quickly bought their lunches, and found seats.

"Good Citizen award," Chloe muttered, shaking her head. Her shoulders slumped as she sipped miserably from her carton of lemonade.

"Hey, lighten up," Riley said. "What's the big deal? I mean, Travis has probably already forgotten about it by now."

Chloe looked up. "You think?" she asked hopefully.

"I'm positive," Riley said. "Now let's talk about something really important – like the party."

Before Chloe could reply, Mr. Conner's voice came over the P.A. system.

"Attention, students," he said. "I'd like everyone to put their hands together for Chloe Carlson, who has once again won the important Good Citizen award!"

"Oooohh!" a bunch of kids at a nearby table chanted, making fun of her.

Chloe wanted to hide. Not only did Travis think the award was lame, so did the whole school!

"I hope everyone learns something from Chloe's fine example," Mr. Conner went on.

Half the people in the cafeteria broke out laughing.

"Ugh!" Chloe groaned, hiding her face in her hands. "I feel like I'm in third grade again!"

"Forget about it," Riley said. "Let's talk about *the party*."

"Oh, no! I just realised something horrible." Chloe spread her fingers and peeked out, glancing around the cafeteria. "Is Travis eating inside or out today? Did he hear the announcement?" she asked. "Did he see everyone laughing at me? Is *he* laughing?"

Riley checked out the cafeteria and nodded. "He's sitting with Kyle and Cameron. Inside. They seem to be laughing about something. Oops! Don't look now – he's watching you. Yeah, I think they're laughing about you."

"Oh, great!" Chloe complained.

"Well, you asked," Riley said. "Anyway, what happened after history class? Did you talk to Travis? Did you mention the party?"

Chloe shook her head and took a bite of her taco. "No. After he heard Conner tell me about the award, he laughed and walked away."

"Well, it *is* pretty funny, you have to admit," Riley said. She picked up a piece of avocado that had fallen out of her tortilla wrap.

"I can't *help* it if I'm reliable and conscientious!" Chloe complained.

"I know," Riley agreed. "Face it, Chloe. You and Travis don't have that much in common. You're a good citizen, and he's in detention so much, he has his mail sent there."

"But that's what makes him so...so...hot!" Chloe argued. "Haven't you heard? Opposites attract. Besides, he's not really so bad. He just gets detention all the time

13

because he's late to class and likes to joke around."

"I still say you two aren't exactly made for each other," Riley insisted.

"I know," Chloe admitted. "And the worst thing is, he doesn't even know I'm alive."

"Nothing new about that," Riley said. "I mean you're always chasing after guys who aren't interested in you."

"Me? You're the one who's always falling for rock stars and movie stars," Chloe argued.

"That's different," Riley insisted. "My fantasy guys are just that — fantasies. I don't kid myself. But *you* go after real-life guys who are just plain not your type."

[Chloe: So maybe she's got a point. I guess it all started when I was about five years old. The Malibu Merry Mermaid Nursery School. His name? Billy Schisler. A rebel. At snack time he refused to drink his milk through a straw. He was sooo cute! I used to finger-paint his name over and over again. All I wanted was one shot with him on the seesaw. But no matter what I did — let him win at Simon Says, squirt grape juice through my missing front teeth — he never gave me the time of day. And it made me sooo crazy.]

"It's going to be hard to get him to really notice you," Riley said. "Maybe the only way is if you get detention, too!"

"Get detention?" Chloe's eyes lit up. "Then I could

14

spend a whole hour with Travis every day after school!"

"I was only *kidding*!" Riley protested.

"But it's a great idea and it just might work," Chloe said.

"Wow. The things we do for love," Riley muttered.

Chloe thought about it for a minute. It would be hard to get detention – it was *so* not her style. She'd have to figure something out. But it was definitely a plan.

"Congratulations on your award," a voice beside Chloe said quietly.

Chloe looked over. It was Amanda, sitting at the end of the table. Was she kidding? Chloe wondered.

Amanda smiled a kind of funny smile. Like she was half-kidding and half-serious. Like she knew the award was dumb, but she also knew that it was sort of nice to get awards, even for stupid stuff.

"Thanks," Chloe said, smiling back.

"Do you want to come over this afternoon?" Amanda asked. "We could start working on our research project for history."

Chloe started to answer, but just then Sarah – a.k.a. Sierra – showed up and plopped down on the bench next to her.

"Hi, guys. What's up?" Sierra asked. "Can I sit here?"

Sierra's real name was Sarah Pomeroy. She was friends with Riley mostly, but Chloe liked her, too.

Sierra was a lot of fun, and a little on the wild side.

Unfortunately, Sierra had really conservative parents. That's why she led a kind of double life. At home, she went by her real name and dressed the way her parents wanted her to – in totally boring sweaters and skirts. As far as they knew, she was a perfect student who got good grades and played the violin.

But at school she transformed herself. She wore tight black jeans and a suede jacket, played bass guitar in a cool band called The Wave, and went by the name Sierra.

"Are you sure you want to be seen with West Malibu High's Good Citizen of the Month?" Chloe asked Sierra.

"I figure if you're such a good citizen, you'll share that brownie with me," Sierra joked, eyeing Chloe's dessert.

"Take it," Chloe said, passing the brownie to Sierra. "I'm too depressed to eat."

Sierra grabbed the brownie happily and stacked it on top of her own.

"How'd you get out of English?" Riley asked, knowing that Sierra didn't have lunch that period.

"I'm supposed to be at the library, but I was too hungry to study. So what's up?" Sierra repeated the question.

"We're planning a party," Riley answered. "For this Friday night."

"You're invited, of course," Chloe added quickly, looking at Sierra. Then she glanced at Amanda, including her. "You should come, too."

"At least we *hope* we're having a party," Riley jumped in. "We haven't actually cleared it with our mom yet. But assuming she says yes— "

"She *has* to say yes," Chloe interrupted. "*Everyone* knows about the party now. I invited Tara and Quinn after second period."

"Okay, let's assume it's definite. But so far, Chloe can't get up the nerve to ask the guy she likes," Riley explained. "And I don't have anybody, either. I need a date for this thing. That's the whole reason we're having the— "

Suddenly a pair of hands grabbed her head and covered her eyes from behind.

"Hey!" Riley cried. "Ow!"

"Guess who?" a guy's voice said.

As if Riley couldn't guess? Chloe thought.

There was only one guy who constantly hung around Riley. Who followed her like a stray puppy. Who showed up at her house at every hour of the day and night.

Larry Slotnick.

Larry, their nerdy next-door neighbour. Larry, who was so madly in love with Riley that he had a collection of all her empty yogurt containers.

"Hi, Larry," Riley said patiently. "Could you not squeeze my head so tight when you do that?"

"How'd you know it was me?" Larry asked.

Riley rolled her eyes. "Sort of the same way I know where my feet are each morning when I put on my shoes."

Larry tilted his head. "Really? How?" he asked.

Sierra laughed. "You're hysterical," she said to Larry.

"So what about this afternoon?" Amanda asked Chloe softly.

Oh, yeah. The research project. I guess I'd better do it today, Chloe decided, since I'm going to try to get detention with Travis tomorrow!

"Okay," she said.

Sierra popped a big chunk of brownie into her mouth.

"You're eating your dessert first," Larry commented.

"I'm eating my dessert *instead*," Sierra replied. "I only took the veggie plate so the cafeteria ladies wouldn't yell at me."

"So, can we talk about Friday?" Chloe asked.

"This is a private conversation," Riley explained to Larry. "So, uh, we'll see you later. Okay?"

"Okay," Larry said. "How much later?"

"Later!" Riley said firmly, but as nicely as she could.

When he was gone, Riley let out a sigh of relief. "Now back to the main topic. Someone has to help me figure out who to invite to the party."

"So what kind of guy are you looking for?" Sierra asked.

Riley thought for a minute. "He's got to be someone nice. Someone fun to be with. Someone better than Daniel Pitowsky."

"Who's Daniel Pitowsky?" Amanda asked quietly.

Chloe turned to Amanda, surprised, but glad, that she had joined in. Maybe she's not as shy as we thought. Or maybe she just needed to feel like we were including her.

"He's a guy I knew in junior high," Riley explained. "He goes to a private school now, but he called me up and asked me out last week. Ugh – it was the worst date of my life. He was so rude."

"I remember him," Sierra said. "He's a creep."

"What happened?" Amanda asked.

"We went to the movies, and he met up with a bunch of his buddies there," Riley explained. "He spent the whole time talking to them instead of me. And he bought himself popcorn, and didn't even offer me any!"

"Anyone would be better than Daniel Pitowsky," Chloe agreed.

"I need someone who's the *opposite* of him," Riley said. "Someone considerate, who actually wants to talk to me. And he has to be funny, too."

Sierra finished her first brownie and brushed the crumbs off her hands. Then she put her palms on her hips and looked Riley in the eye. "Listen," Sierra said. "I know a guy who's exactly what you're looking for."

"Really?" Riley asked, interested. "Tell me more!"

Sierra sighed. "He's so sweet. He'd walk you home, carry your books…and there's no doubt he'd make you laugh," she replied. "And from what I've heard, I think he has a crush on you."

Wow, Chloe thought. He sounds perfect for her!

"You're kidding!" Riley cried. "What's his name?"

"I'm not sure if I should tell you," Sierra said. "Are you really open to suggestions?"

"Definitely!" Riley said. "If he's that nice, I'd go out with him in a heartbeat! Who is he?"

chapter three

Riley could barely stand the suspense. If Sierra had the perfect guy in mind, why didn't she just spit it out?

"It's Larry," Sierra said matter-of-factly. And she shot Riley a look that said, "You should have figured it out yourself."

"Larry? Are you kidding?" Riley cried. "He's my worst nightmare!"

"No way!" Sierra argued. "I mean, I *know* the downside. He follows you constantly, he's a little goofy, and you've known him practically your whole life. But that's why you're missing it. I mean, I think Larry is sort of interesting."

"Interesting? You mean the way the slime from slugs is interesting?" Riley asked.

"Oh, come on," Chloe objected. "Larry is *not* a slug."

"Okay, he's not a slug. But he's definitely not boyfriend material," Riley said.

"Why not?" Sierra asked. "I mean, he's totally nuts about you. If you'd give him half a chance, he'd treat you like royalty. And just think, if it worked out, he'd be an instant boyfriend!"

Instant boyfriend? With the party coming up, Riley liked the sound of that. Maybe she *should* give him a chance. Maybe Sierra was right. Maybe Larry *did* have a lot of great qualities. She just couldn't think of any!

"You're missing out on a good thing," Sierra said as she started on her second brownie. "At least give Larry a chance and see how it works out."

"I don't know," Riley said slowly. She certainly wasn't going to make any promises. Larry was nice, but he could act so unbelievably weird sometimes. On the other hand, if Sierra thought he was cool…maybe Riley *was* missing something.

"I'll think about it," Riley agreed half-heartedly.

"So what time is the party?" Amanda asked.

"We haven't worked out the details yet," Riley answered.

"Yeah – details like getting permission to have the party at all," Chloe mumbled. "Or planning the decorations, buying the food, or figuring out what to wear. And we've only got five days to do it!"

Riley stood to dump the trash from her lunch tray. It was almost time for class to start.

"Catch you later," Sierra called, still nibbling on her second brownie.

On the way to the trash bin, someone from Riley's biology class tapped her on the shoulder. "So you're having a party?" the girl asked. "So cool! What time?"

News travels fast, Riley thought. She hardly even knew this girl! "Uh, we're not sure about the time," Riley answered.

"Is it dressy or casual?" the girl asked. "And can I bring someone?"

"Um, I don't know," Riley said. "Ask me tomorrow. We're still in the planning stages."

"Okay, but I already told Natalie and Kevin and Kyle about it," the girl said. "See you!" She dashed off to join a bunch of kids who were hanging around, waiting for the bell to ring.

Riley started to follow her, but as she got closer she heard them all talking about the party, too. She took a detour and headed to her locker.

I hope Mom doesn't have a problem with this party, Riley thought. A ton of people already know about it. It will be really hard to call it off.

Riley spun the dial on her locker, mumbling the combination.

"Thirteen…eight…umm…why can't I ever remember these stupid numbers?" she muttered.

From inside her locker, a voice called out, "Twenty-two."

Riley gasped. Then she spun the dial. She knew that voice. She yanked open the locker door. Larry was wedged into the small space, and grinning out at her.

"Hi!" he said brightly.

"Larry, what are you doing in my locker?" she demanded.

"I wanted to surprise you with the good news," Larry said.

"Let me guess," Riley said. "You're going to get beamed back up to the mothership?"

"No." Larry shook his head, still grinning. He looked like he could hardly wait to tell her. "We – as in you and me – are going to be lab partners in biology!"

[Riley: Me and Larry bio partners? I can just see it now. Larry pulls me into the lab. A wild look flashes into his eyes as he slams the door shut – and locks it. Sitting in the middle of the room is a strange chair, with huge metal clamps on the arms and legs. "I'm going to create the perfect woman!" he says, cackling and slipping on a white lab coat. He clamps me into the chair. "Don't be afraid. Frankenstein had his bride – and I will have mine! Ah-ha-ha-ha-ha-ha!"]

"Noooo!" Riley screamed.

"What's wrong? We're just going to dissect a frog together," Larry said. "Is this going to be great or what?"

Riley pulled herself together and tried to stay calm. Remember what Sierra said, she told herself. Give him a chance. If it works, it could be great.

"Uh, yeah, that's wonderful," Riley said. "Well, we'd better get going – *partner*. We have bio next period."

"Okay, yeah," Larry answered, sounding worried. "There's only one thing."

"What?" Riley asked.

"I can't get out," Larry admitted.

Perfect, Riley thought. What an ideal boyfriend! Someone you have to pry out of your locker with a crowbar!

She took Larry's hand and gave him a yank. He didn't even wince as his shoulder scraped on the locker opening.

At least he's not a whiner, Riley thought.

And just as Sierra predicted, he carried her books to class. "After you," Larry said, like a perfect gentleman, letting her go first into the lab room.

Riley took a seat in the back and Larry sat down beside her. For the next fifty minutes, he didn't do one goofy or geeky thing.

"Mint?" Larry offered when class was over.

This is nice, Riley thought. Strange…but nice. And who knows? Maybe Sierra is right. Maybe I should give him a chance.

"Thanks," she said, taking a mint from the tin he was holding. "Listen, I was thinking. Since we're lab partners on this frog project, do you want to come over after school today for a study date?"

"Date?" Larry said, practically falling all over her. "Are you serious? Did.you just say the word *date*?"

"Calm down, Larry. It's not *that* big a deal," she said.

"Okay, okay," Larry said. "I'm calm. It's just that I'd totally *love* to have a study date with you – but I can't today. I have a dentist appointment after school."

"Oh," Riley said.

This is so weird, she thought. He's turning *me* down – and I'm actually disappointed.

"I mean, if it were anything else, I'd just cancel the appointment," Larry went on. "But I've got to go today because my brace is all messed up. I think I used it too many times as a hockey puck."

Riley winced. "That's kind of gross, Larry."

"Want to see it?" Larry offered. He started to reach into his pocket.

"No!" Riley put up her hands like a traffic cop. "That's okay. We'll do it another time," she said.

"How about tomorrow?" Larry begged.

"Okay, whatever. Tomorrow," Riley promised as she hurried down the hall. But deep down she had a feeling that giving Larry a chance was going to be a disaster – no matter what Sierra said.

chapter
four

"**W**ow. I like your room," Chloe said as she tossed her backpack on the floor in Amanda's room that afternoon.

Amanda's house wasn't on the beach like Chloe's. It was in a woodsy neighbourhood, surrounded by tall redwoods. All the floors were made of wide pine boards, highly polished. Amanda's big corner bedroom windows looked out on a thick patch of trees.

"Yeah, it's pretty private back here," Amanda agreed.

"Did you decorate it yourself?" Chloe asked.

Amanda nodded. "I thought about having a pink and green room, but it just didn't go with the house or the woods. So my mom and I picked out all this antique pine furniture and the quilts."

"Cool," Chloe said. "I love quilts."

"Me, too," Amanda replied. "But don't you wish you could have two or three different bedrooms, so you could decorate each one a completely different way?"

"Totally," Chloe agreed. "I thought I was going to get to do that when my mom and dad decided to separate for a while. But then my dad moved into a trailer on the beach."

"Really?" Amanda asked. "That's kind of cool."

Chloe nodded. "It's fun sometimes, except Riley and I didn't exactly get new rooms of our own. But we've done *amazing* things with the sofa bed," she joked.

Amanda laughed and flipped the switch on her computer as she sat down at her desk. "So about this history project. I figured we could do most of the research online."

"Excellent," Chloe said, flopping down on her stomach on Amanda's bed. "Let's go for it."

"What's the topic?" Amanda asked.

"Causes of the Boston Tea Party," Chloe reminded her with a huge sigh. "How did *we* get stuck with that one?"

"Don't ask me," Amanda said. "I'm a coffee drinker myself."

Chloe laughed. Wow. She had no idea that Amanda was so funny.

Maybe Amanda felt more comfortable because she was at home, on her own turf. Maybe that's why she felt that she could open up a little, and that they could talk more. Whatever the reason, Chloe was glad that she was getting to know her.

Amanda clicked her mouse a few times and started searching the Internet.

Chloe stared at the monitor. The website was slow. It can't hurt to read something while we're waiting, she thought. She reached into her backpack and pulled out her history book.

Amanda turned around in her chair and spotted the fashion magazine that was inside Chloe's backpack. "Is that this month's *Scene*?" she asked.

"Yup." Chloe pulled it out. She jumped off the bed and handed it to Amanda.

"The clothes this season are sort of the same as last year, only brighter," Amanda said, flipping through the pages. "I wish they'd come up with something else."

"Yeah," Chloe agreed. She leaned over Amanda's shoulder. "Still, some of the outfits are cute." She pointed to a girl wearing an orange sweater with bell sleeves. "Like that one. I bet you would look incredible in that."

"Maybe." Amanda turned the page.

"Hey, check that out." It was a two-page spread on the latest hairstyles. One photo showed a girl who looked a lot like Amanda, with her hair in an assortment of loose braids all over her head.

Amanda glanced at the magazine and nodded. "Nice."

"That would look so great on you!" Chloe said. "Can I try it?"

"Why not?" Amanda shrugged. "I'm sitting here anyway,

waiting for this stupid search engine to find Boston Tea Party. We can be multi-tasking!"

Chloe grabbed a brush from Amanda's dresser and started separating her hair into strands. "How long have you lived here?" she asked Amanda.

"A little over a year," Amanda said. "I used to live on a hill in San Francisco. From our living room, we could see the water in three directions. So this is a total change for me."

Hmm, Chloe thought. It wouldn't be much fun to move – and leave all your friends behind – right before your freshman year in high school.

Amanda's computer announced, "You've got mail."

"Hang on," Amanda said. "I've got to read this. It's from my friends back home."

"Should I go away?" Chloe offered, letting Amanda's hair drop. "You know, give you some privacy?"

"No, keep going," she said, gesturing to the braids.

Chloe separated more pieces of hair into strands, following the photo in the magazine. She glanced over Amanda's shoulder at the computer screen.

"Yes!" Amanda shouted. "Look. My friend Molly sent me a picture of Jason!"

Chloe leaned in to get a better look at the picture. A really cute guy grinned out at them from the screen. He had short tufts of sun-bleached brown hair, similar to Travis's.

"Is that your boyfriend?" Chloe asked.

"No," Amanda said, sounding embarrassed. "More like my best guy-friend," she said. "We used to play Ultimate Frisbee together."

"He's definitely hot," Chloe said, thinking more about Travis than the guy whose picture was on the screen.

"Um-hmm," Amanda said. "He looks like that guy who rode his dirt bike in the hall a few weeks ago. What's his name? The one who's always getting detention?"

In the silence, Chloe was trying to decide whether to tell Amanda about her crush. But she didn't have to make up her mind.

"You like him, don't you?" Amanda asked, turning to face Chloe.

"How did you know?" Chloe asked.

"I kind of saw you stumble into that locker after class today, so I figured it out. Major crush city?"

Chloe nodded. "His name's Travis. And yeah – I'm so into him I can't think straight!"

Amanda laughed. "Or walk straight," she said. "So...how come you like him?"

Chloe could tell it was a serious question: what did she actually *like* about Travis?

"Well, he's such a free spirit, you know?" Chloe said. "I mean, he gets in trouble a lot – sure. But it's not because he's really bad. He just seems to be willing to break a few of the dumber rules, to make life a bit more interesting."

Amanda nodded. "Makes sense to me," she said.

This is cool, Chloe thought. It was nice to have a new friend who talked about stuff like it really mattered.

"So what are you going to do? I mean, are you asking him to your party on Friday night?" Amanda asked.

Chloe flopped back down on the bed and moaned. "That's the whole problem," she said. "I want to, but I barely see him around school. Besides, he doesn't seem to know I'm alive! So I have a plan." Her eyes lit up and she leaned forward to confide in Amanda. "I'm going to think of a way to get detention tomorrow after school. That way, he *can't* ignore me. What do you think?"

"I think you're not the detention type," Amanda said.

"So?" Chloe argued. "I can change. I've got to. I mean, I'm willing to do whatever it takes to get his attention."

Amanda pinched her lips tight as if she didn't want to say anything more. But then she did. "Look, I just don't think you should change for anyone. I think you should be yourself. What's wrong with *that* plan?"

"He'll never notice me," Chloe said. "*That's* what's wrong with that plan. I've got to do something to sort of level the playing field. Meet him on his own turf, you know what I mean?"

Amanda shrugged. "If you say so. But how are you going to get detention?"

Chloe giggled. "I don't know. At first I was thinking I could bring our new puppy to school. That should get me into trouble – she's not completely housebroken. But that's too wimpy."

"Definitely," Amanda said. "Anyway, they wouldn't give you detention for that. They'd just send you home. You need something *really* bad. Like sneaking into the cafeteria and putting cayenne pepper in all the food."

Chloe's eyes lit up. "Or better yet, how about just in Mr. Conner's coffee? I hear he's a zombie in the morning until he has his coffee. A little cayenne would really wake him up!"

"That's good," Amanda said. "The only problem is, how would he know *you* did it?"

"Hmm," Chloe said. "Good point. But that's the problem with a lot of my ideas. I was thinking I could shaving-cream Conner's car, but how would he know it was me?"

"From the handwriting?" Amanda teased. "I mean, you *do* have very neat handwriting – as any model citizen would."

Chloe rolled her eyes. "Come on. You're not helping. We're trying to make me look *bad*. When I'm led into detention and Travis Morgan leans over and asks, 'What are you in for?' I want to tell him something that rocks!"

"Okay, okay, I've got it," Amanda said. "You show up at school in chains and leather and start stealing people's cars!"

"Whoa," Chloe said. "I'm only trying to get detention – not ten years in jail!"

"Well," Amanda said with a shrug. "You could always fall back on my original idea, and just be yourself around Travis."

"Nope," Chloe said. "I've got to get detention. But I think I'll just keep it simple."

"You have an idea," Amanda said. "I can tell from the sneaky look on your face."

Chloe nodded. "I just thought of it. And it's an oldie but goodie. Yes, I know exactly what I'm going to do!"

chapter
five

"Poor baby. No study date with Larry?" Sierra teased. "What a bummer!"

Riley and Sierra walked down a narrow stone path between two stucco houses.

"Shhh!" Riley said. "I'm not even sure how I feel about this whole Larry thing, so I'm not telling anyone about it yet. I mean, it might not even work out."

"I'm cool," Sierra said as she rang the bell at the back door of Alex's house.

Alex was the lead guitarist in Sierra's band. Sometimes he sang, too. The band rehearsed a couple of days a week, after school. Usually they hung out at Saul's house, since he was the drummer, and drums were hard to move. But this week they were at Alex's. Sierra had invited Riley to hang out during their rehearsal.

"Come on in," Alex's mother said, opening the back door. "They're all downstairs."

Riley took a seat on a low couch at the back of the basement and put her feet up on an old coffee table. Sierra dropped her school stuff in a heap.

"Sierra, listen to this," Alex said while Sierra plugged in her bass guitar and amp. He counted off the numbers and the drummer started playing. "One, two, one-two-three-four," Alex said, nodding his head on each count.

The song had a sad, mellow feel but a hard, driving beat. Alex sang the first four lines:

"Never let the night escape. Never wait for day to break. Never let her make you ache. Never lie and never fake...."

Wow, Riley thought. That's really good.

She watched Alex as he sang it, closing his eyes slightly and bending his body back and forth.

Why didn't I ever notice him before? she wondered. Because he's so quiet. Quieter than everyone else in the band.

There were four of them in the group: Sierra, Alex, Marta, and Saul. And a backing singer named Josh was trying to join. According to Sierra, though, they hadn't decided whether to let him in.

Riley watched the band members, one by one, remembering the stuff Sierra had told her about them.

Saul was a complete goof. He kept interrupting the rehearsal to tell them the plots of all the shows he saw on the Cartoon Network.

Marta played keyboards, and sometimes she mixed

records when they wanted a hip-hop sound. But she wasn't there today. Sierra said that Marta couldn't be counted on to show up for all the rehearsals.

Josh was telling everybody how to play their instruments. He's acting like he's the lead singer, Riley thought. He seemed to be pretty full of himself. It takes a lot of nerve to act as if he's in charge or something, when he isn't even in the band yet! she realised.

And then there was Alex. Alex with the sandy-blond hair that sort of hung over his dark brown eyes.

Yeah. He's quiet, Riley thought again.

But that wasn't totally true. He was talking right now, telling Saul how to make the song better.

"We need more bass drum when we kick it off," Alex said. "Can you hit it a little harder on one and three?"

"You got it," Saul nodded. He kept fiddling with his cymbals the whole time.

Alex tuned his guitar. "Want to try it again?"

He's really the leader of the group, Riley realized. But he's so quiet about it – not pushy, not in anyone's face. It's as though they hardly notice that he's running the show.

Before he counted it off this time, he glanced over at Riley. For a second, their eyes locked. The corner of his mouth turned up. Almost a smile.

Riley felt her heartbeat pick up a little.

"This one's for all our fans out there in the audience," Alex joked, since Riley was the only person there.

Then he started the song again, slow and sad, closing his eyes and leaning in really close to the mike.

Riley stared at him, totally riveted. When she glanced away, Sierra was watching her watch him.

I know what she's thinking, Riley thought. She can tell I like him.

[**Riley: Okay, don't say it. I know what you're thinking: What about Larry? But you and I both know that it would never work out between Larry and me. I mean, I don't know why I listened to Sierra in the first place. I like Larry, but only as a friend. A good friend. That's why I'm going through with the study date tomorrow. I made a promise to him, and I'm not going to break it. I wouldn't want to hurt his feelings.**]

Alex strummed his guitar hard on the last two chords, and the song was over.

"Okay, that was rough," Sierra said. "But it's going to be killer when we get it together."

"Right." Josh turned to Alex. "Next time, sing it like you mean it, man. I mean, for real."

"Time for a break. We need munchies!" Saul shouted, dropping his sticks and leaping up to raid the small fridge they had in the basement.

"That was great," Riley said. She stood up to get something to drink, too.

"You liked it?" Alex asked shyly.

"I thought it was really awesome," she replied.

"I don't know. I think it needs something else," Alex said, looking down at the chords he was still fingering. Then he slowly raised his eyes to hers. "Got any ideas?"

Riley smiled. Was he flirting with her? Because if he was, she wanted to flirt back! "How about a kazoo on the ending?" she joked.

"That could work for me," Alex said, giving her a shy smile. "Uh, but I don't know. Every band in Malibu has a kazoo. Maybe we should brainstorm about this some more."

"Okay, sure," Riley said because she couldn't think of anything else to say.

"How about tomorrow after school?" Alex asked. "We could meet at California Dream, get some mochas, and figure something out."

A date? With Alex? At California Dream? That sounded like heaven. And if it worked out, she could even ask him to the party for Friday!

Riley started to say yes instantly. But then she remembered that she already *had* a date for tomorrow. A study date – with Larry.

It wouldn't be right to back out just because she got a better offer, Riley decided.

"Uh, I can't," she said, sort of stumbling.

Quick – think of an excuse! Anything! Riley told herself. She didn't want to tell Alex about Larry. She didn't want him to get the wrong idea.

"Oh. Okay," Alex said, looking very disappointed.

"But maybe we could..." Riley started.

Maybe we could do it another day, she was trying to say. But before the words came out, someone clomped down the basement steps and bounced into the room.

"Surprise!" Larry cried, spreading his arms wide as if he thought Riley might actually run over and give him a hug.

"Larry?" Riley said. "What are you doing here?"

"Hi," Larry said, nodding to everyone in the band. Then he grinned at Riley. "I got finished early with the orthodontist, and Manuelo told me you were here."

Manuelo was the live-in housekeeper who worked for Riley's mom. He cooked, he cleaned, and he put his two-cents worth in on most of their problems. In other words, he was part of the family.

"Yup. I'm here," Riley said. Note to self, she thought, remind Manuelo *not* to give Larry so much information!

"So, I got my brace fixed," Larry announced. He took it out of his pocket and offered to pass it around. "Want to see? That big gouge there was from a game of air hockey. But they put some plastic fixative on it, so I'm good to go."

"Dude, get that thing away from me!" Saul said, backing away from the brace.

"Larry, you want some crisps?" Sierra offered, trying to be nice and change the subject.

"Nah, that's okay. I just came over to get Riley. We've got a study date for tomorrow, but I thought, hey, maybe we can get started early. Like today!"

Riley glanced at Alex. She wanted to explain the whole thing to him. To tell Alex that there was nothing going on with Larry. But how could she say it in front of Larry, without hurting his feelings?

Please don't jump to the wrong conclusion, she said silently. Please! It was too late. The minute she saw the look on Alex's face, she knew. Jump to the wrong conclusion? He already had!

"Alex?" Riley said, moving towards him.

But he didn't answer. He picked up his guitar, turned his back to her, and started playing.

"Let's get back to work," he said to the rest of the band.

chapter six

"**C**an you believe it?" Riley said later that night. She had just finished explaining the rehearsal episode to Chloe – including the part about Larry coming in at totally the wrong time. "So now I have no idea what to do."

"Simple. Just ask Alex to the party," Chloe advised her.

"How?" Riley asked. "He wouldn't even talk to me. Besides, he'll probably say no. He thinks I'm going out with Larry!"

"Then call Alex and tell him you're not," Chloe replied. "Tell him you were just having a study date with Larry."

"I don't even want to go have that study date with Larry," Riley said. "And I don't think Sierra's right. I don't think Larry is boyfriend material." She sighed. "But what if she *is* right?" She started pacing the room, twisting her hands together. "Oh, Chloe, this is such a mess. You've got to help me!"

Chloe closed her eyes and held her head. "Okay, here's what you do," she told her sister. "If the study date goes amazingly well, then ask Larry to the party."

"But – " Riley began.

Chloe held up her hand to stop her. "If not, then let Larry down easily. And give Alex a call."

"But what if Alex turns *me* down?" Riley said again.

"You're talking in circles!" Chloe complained. "Just take it one day at a time. We'll come up with something if that happens."

Riley nodded. "Okay. Sounds like a plan – I guess."

Phew! Chloe thought. And I think I've got problems with Travis. At least I'm only dealing with one guy!

"Now all we have to do is ask Mom if we can have the party," Riley said.

"Details," Chloe muttered as she and her sister hurried downstairs.

The girls found their mother lying on the sofa in the living room with her feet propped up on the sofa back. She was talking to a client on the cordless phone.

"Mom, we need to talk," Chloe whispered.

Macy Carlson held up one finger to say, "Just a sec."

"That's the trouble with having a mom who works at home," Chloe mumbled. "She never leaves the office."

Chloe and Riley's mom was a fashion designer. She and their dad had worked together for years. Now that they were separated, she was handling the business on her own.

A minute later Macy covered the mouthpiece of the phone and glanced up at them. "What? Ask me quickly," she said. "I've got a big fish on the line."

"Can we have a party?" Chloe asked. "We're thinking about twenty or thirty – "

"Sure, whatever," their mother interrupted. "Just talk to Manuelo about it." Then she went back to her phone call.

"Whoa. That was easy," Chloe said.

"She didn't even flinch when you said thirty people!" Riley whispered excitedly.

"I know." Chloe giggled. "Maybe we should have gone for forty!"

"The way Rebecca's spreading the word, we'll be lucky to keep it under fifty," Riley admitted.

Manuelo was in the kitchen, cutting up mangos to make his special salsa.

"Manuelo, we're having a party this Friday, and Mom said to talk to you about it," Chloe began.

"Oh, yes, yes, yes," Manuelo said. "What do you think of Cuban sandwiches, crisps and *queso*, and lots of Latin music? And I thought we could string paper lanterns outside, on the deck facing the beach. It will be so romantic."

"Cool!" Chloe said. "But how did you come up with that so fast?"

"They don't call me Latin Lightning for nothing!" Manuelo joked.

Wow, Chloe thought. This party is going to be so hot! Now all I have to do is get Travis's attention – which means getting detention.

And tomorrow is the big day.

She hurried upstairs to find something fabulous to wear to school. Something that would stay wrinkle free all the way through last period!

"So don't wait for me after school," Chloe told Riley as they strolled towards the front steps of West Malibu High the next morning.

"Why not?" Riley asked.

"Because if all goes according to plan, I'll be doing an hour's worth of detention today."

"You're really going to do it?" Riley asked. She pushed her straight blonde hair back off her shoulders.

Chloe nodded. "I've got it all worked out. I just hope Mr. Conner wears something washable."

"Hold on, walk slower – there's Alex," Riley said under her breath. "Maybe he'll talk to me."

Chloe slowed down and both girls tried to act casual. Alex was sitting on the front steps, bent over a small black notebook, writing something.

"Is he looking at me?" Riley asked.

"He's not even looking up," Chloe answered softly. "You're going to have to make the first move."

"No, I can't do that. He seems way too into whatever he's writing," Riley said.

"You're right," Chloe said. She watched Alex for another minute. He kept writing, then scratching things out the whole time. Then, out of the corner of her eye, she saw a group of her friends coming towards her.

"Oh, there's Quinn. I'll catch you later," Chloe said, splitting off from her sister.

Chloe caught up with Quinn and Tara. They were all psyched about the party. Tara had already gone out and bought a new dress to wear.

"I'm going shopping tonight," Chloe announced. "I think I've got enough money for that shimmery little red dress in the window at Babette's."

"Cool," Quinn said. "But what about shoes?"

Shoes are a problem, Chloe thought. But the bigger problem was Travis. Getting *him* to the party was much more important than getting new shoes!

The bell rang and Chloe saw Amanda hurrying up a side walkway with her backpack slung over one shoulder.

"Hey," Chloe called, catching up with her.

"Hey," Amanda answered. "If I fall asleep in history today, kick me or something. I am *so* tired."

"How come?" Chloe asked.

"I got hooked on *Buffy* reruns," Amanda admitted. "And then I had to stay up late to finish my homework."

"I think you could probably sleep through most of Ms. Simmons's class and she'd never notice," Chloe joked as they headed into the school building together.

On the way, Chloe checked out Amanda's hair. It was brushed straight, not up in the braids like in the magazine.

"What happened to your hair?" Chloe asked.

"Huh?" Amanda reached up, feeling the top of her head. "Did my little brother put silly string in it again? I'm gonna *kill* him!"

"No, no," Chloe said. "The braids. They looked so awesome on you yesterday, I thought maybe you'd put it up again yourself."

"No time," Amanda said. "I woke up late."

"Oh, right," Chloe said. "But you really should try it at school. I bet you'd get a lot of attention." She paused. "In a good way."

"Thanks," Amanda said. "Maybe I will someday."

Chloe reached into her backpack. "Listen, I want you to try this," she said, handing a lip gloss to Amanda. "I bought this a few weeks ago, but it doesn't really work for me. I have a feeling that it will look great on you, though."

Amanda laughed as if she thought it was funny that Chloe was doing all these things for her. But she quickly applied the lip gloss to her lips.

"It's awesome!" Chloe said. "I knew it would be."

"Really?" Amanda asked.

"Definitely. That colour is totally perfect. Why don't you keep it?" Chloe said.

"Oh, no, I couldn't!" Amanda protested. "I mean, it's yours."

"No, really," Chloe insisted. "I want you to have it."

"Um, okay." Amanda dropped the lip gloss into her bag, but she had a funny look on her face. "See you at lunch," she said as they reached her homeroom.

"Wish me luck – that's when I'm going to do it!" Chloe said.

"Do what?" Amanda asked.

"Get detention," Chloe whispered. Then she hurried down the hall.

But by the time lunch period rolled around, Chloe was starting to lose her nerve. This is a crazy plan, she thought as she paced in front of the soda machine, just inside the cafeteria.

She knew for a fact that Mr. Conner bought a Diet Coke from it, at fourth period, every single day. When he came by, Chloe would offer to buy him one. Then she'd shake it up, open it, and squirt it right in his face. He'd slap her with detention for sure!

I just hate to get his clothes all sticky, Chloe thought.

Her knees were shaking as Mr. Conner marched up to the soda machine. "H-hi, Mr. Conner. Can I, um, buy you a soda?" she asked with a smile.

"Oh, no thanks, Chloe," Mr. Conner replied.

No? Chloe repeated silently. She hadn't counted on him saying *no*. What should I do now? she wondered. My plan totally depends on buying him a can of soda!

She watched Mr. Conner put some coins in the drink machine. He pushed a button, but nothing happened. "Well, would you look at that?" he muttered. "It ate my money again!"

"No problem." Chloe rushed to help. "I'll get this machine to spit out a soda for you." She started kicking the machine as hard as she could.

Mr. Conner watched, amazed. "I had no idea you were so strong, Chloe. Maybe you should consider joining our soccer team."

Finally a can of soda dropped into the chute with a thunk.

"There," Chloe said, grabbing the soda for Mr. Conner before he could reach it. She pretended she was going to hand it to him, then stopped. "Oh no, Mr. Conner, look! Those kids are throwing meatballs!"

The vice principal whirled around to see what Chloe was pointing at. While his back was turned, she quickly shook the can. Now all she had to do was squirt the soda in his face.

"Where?" Mr. Conner was asking. "I don't see anyone throwing anything."

"My mistake," Chloe said as she tried to open the can. But the tab was on too tight. It wouldn't come off!

"Let me help you." A boy named Derrick Malone came by and reached for the can. He pulled off the tab just as Mr. Conner turned around.

so little time

Sticky soda sprayed in the vice principal's face and down the front of his suit. His thin greasy hair was drenched, his glasses were covered, and his shirt was soaked!

"Was that supposed to be *funny*?" Mr. Conner barked at Derrick.

"I didn't do it!" Derrick cried. "I swear!"

"He's right," Chloe broke in. "It's my fault. I shook the can."

Mr. Conner rolled his eyes. "Oh, come on, Chloe. You don't expect me to believe that a good student like you would pull a stupid prank like that. Let's go, Malone," he told the boy. "My office. Move it. And you've got detention, buddy – for the rest of the week."

"No!" Chloe cried. "You've got the wrong person!"

"That's enough, Chloe," Mr. Conner said.

"But…" Chloe's voice trailed off as Mr. Connor dragged Derrick to his office.

"Oh, no," Chloe moaned. "I didn't get detention." Well, there's four days till the party, she thought. Time to come up with plan B – and quick!

chapter
seven

"You look so cute, Riley!" Manuelo said, sort of cooing in his thick Spanish accent. "What are you all dressed up for?"

"Dressed up? This old thing?" Riley answered.

She gazed down at the short hot-pink-and-orange print skirt she was wearing, and the cute little top.

"Old?" Manuelo said, cocking his head. "The price tag is still hanging on it."

"Oops," Riley said, grabbing a pair of scissors to cut it off. "Okay, so I'm dressed up a little. For my study date with Larry. What time is it, anyway? He should be here by now."

"Larry?" Manuelo asked. "You mean the boy who lives next door to us? I thought you avoided him like the plague."

[Riley: **You're wondering why in the world would I dress up for Larry, right? Well, Chloe always**

says, "If you look good, you feel good. And when
you feel good, good things happen." I'm hoping
she's right, and this study date won't be as bad
as I think it will. Wish me luck!]

Riley sighed. "It's a long story, Manuelo," she said.
"Trust me. You don't want to get into the details."

"Well, good luck, Riley," Manuelo said. "I'm going
shopping before we all *starve* to death. We are totally out
of guavas."

Whatever, Riley thought with a laugh. *You're* the only
person in this house who eats guavas.

Manuelo opened the front door. Larry was standing
there with his books in his arms and a backpack on the
ground.

"Larry?" Riley said, surprised. "How long have you
been standing there?"

"Two hours," Larry said. "I don't think your doorbell
works."

Oh, boy, Riley thought. Why didn't he just knock?

"So may I come in?" Larry asked.

"Sure," Riley said.

[**Riley**: Time out. Is that really Larry – or someone
just dressed up in a Larry suit? That's the first
time he actually waited to be asked in! Half the
time he just shows up at our house, uninvited.
Once we came home from a two-week vacation
and he was sitting on the couch, watching TV,

waiting for me to arrive. My mom thought it was
great, because while we were gone he fed the
fish and watered our plants.]

"So, uh, where do you want to work?" Larry asked
with a shy smile.

"How about the couch?" Riley suggested.

She had already put out some crisps, dip, and carrot
sticks for them to munch on.

Larry politely waited for Riley to sit down. Then he
took a seat on the couch beside her.

This is good, Riley thought. So far he hadn't spat
while talking, hadn't tripped, and hadn't broken anything.
He was getting a B plus.

Riley and Chloe's new puppy, Pepper, trotted in and
sniffed at the food on the coffee table.

"No, no, Pepper," Riley said, shooing the dog away.
"That's not for you."

"Is it for us?" Larry asked, eyeing the snack tray.

"Yup. We're going to be hitting the books, so I figure
we'll probably get hungry," Riley said.

Larry reached into his backpack. "Great! Good thing
I brought my spray cheese."

He pulled out a can of aerosol cheese and shot a
long, gooey stream of orange goop into his open mouth.

Ew! He's down to a C plus, Riley thought.

"Want a blast?" Larry offered, holding out the can.

C minus!

"You know, Larry, maybe this was a mistake," Riley said. "Maybe we should study together – over the phone."

"But then you wouldn't get to know Herbie," Larry said, glancing towards his backpack.

Herbie? Who's Herbie? Riley wondered.

Then she heard it: a sound coming from Larry's backpack.

Ribbet. Ribbet.

"Larry, what was that?" Riley asked, scooting away. "Please tell me it was your stomach."

"It's our frog," Larry said.

"*Our* frog?" Riley scooted back even more. "You mean from the bio lab?"

Larry nodded. He reached into his backpack and pulled out the little green frog.

Pepper immediately started barking.

"Larry, that's totally against the rules," Riley said. "Mine *and* the school's!"

Larry looked hurt. "But tomorrow we're going to pin him to a metal tray and...you know. Dissect him. Don't you think he deserves to get out and party a little first?"

"Party?" Riley laughed. She couldn't help it. "Oh, right," she said, joking. "Why don't we put on some music."

Larry thought about it. "Okay," he said. "He could do a little hip-hop."

Riley had to admit the joke was cute. But having a frog in her house wasn't. She knew her mom wouldn't like it one bit.

Besides, Pepper wouldn't stop barking at the frog.

"Larry, you've got to get Herbie out of here," Riley said.

Before he could, the front door opened and Chloe strolled in.

"What's going on?" she asked. Her eyes locked on the thing in Larry's hands. "Is that a *frog*?"

"Shh! Larry sneaked it out of the bio lab," Riley explained.

"What? Do you know how much trouble you can get into for that?" Chloe cried. "That's automatic detention!" She froze. "Detention?" she repeated. A smile crossed her face.

Riley locked eyes with her sister. "No way, Chloe," she said. "Don't you dare."

"Larry, give me that thing!" Chloe lunged for the frog in his hands.

Larry pulled back, trying to protect Herbie from Chloe's attack. In the scuffle, he dropped the frog.

It quickly hopped out of sight.

"Oh, no!" Riley cried. "It escaped!"

Riley, Chloe, and Larry all dropped to their knees, hunting for the frog. Pepper dug at the rug, sniffing wildly. Then she poked her nose at Larry's open backpack.

"Whoa!" Riley cried. "What was that? I just saw something green hop out of your— "

"Oh, no," Larry cried. "They're *all* getting loose!"

"All?" Chloe and Riley both shrieked at once. "What do you mean *all*?"

"I mean, I thought I'd give the little guys from the lab a field trip," Larry admitted as several small frogs hopped around the room.

Riley panicked and lunged for one. But it slipped out of her hands.

"Here, froggie. I mean, froggies!" Chloe called.

"Here, Herbie. Come on, guys. I've got a nice big juicy dead fly for you," Larry said, crawling around.

"Don't lie to them," Riley scolded. "That's not nice."

"I'm not lying," Larry held out his hand for her to see the big dead fly in it.

"Where did you get that?" Riley cringed.

"Caught it on my tongue," Larry said, darting his tongue in and out like a reptile.

"Riley? Chloe? Larry?" Macy Carlson said, her voice rising as she walked into the room. "What on earth is going on!"

"Mom, I— " Riley started to explain. But what could she say? There were frogs everywhere. Pepper was barking and chasing them. Chloe was screaming. Larry was grabbing at the frogs – and missing. It was total chaos!

What was I thinking? Riley wondered, staring at Larry, who was now trying to lure the frogs into his backpack with the dead fly. Why did I ever ask him on a study date in the first place?

• • •

Riley sat at her desk that night, sending Instant Messages back and forth with Sierra.

> RILEY241: It's all your fault. And now we have frogs all over the house!
>
> SIERRA-LALA: Frogs? Plural?????
>
> RILEY241: Yeah. He decided to liberate all the frogs from the bio lab! They were in his backpack, but they escaped.
>
> RILEY241: Hold on. My phone's ringing. Be right back.

Riley picked up the phone beside her bed. "Hello?" she said.

"It's me," Sierra said over the phone. "I can't type about frogs. Are you kidding? What happened? Can't you find them?"

"We found most of them," Riley said. "But one of them is still hiding in my bedroom. I can hear it ribbeting right now!"

"That is so stupid," Sierra said. "How could he do something like that?"

"At least I didn't get grounded, but my mom is totally upset," Riley added. "Anyway, this thing with Larry is *so* not working out."

"I get that," Sierra said. "But maybe it's just that he acts goofy because he's always trying to impress you."

Riley tilted her head. "No. Somehow I'm pretty sure Larry's weird all the time."

"Okay, okay," Sierra said. "Sorry I made you go out with a guy you're not interested in."

"That's okay," Riley said. "But maybe you can help me ask Alex to the party. Can you arrange to have a band practise tomorrow after school – and invite me again?"

"Sure," Sierra agreed. "That's easy. But are you sure you want to dump Larry? I mean, if things don't work out with Alex, maybe you'll end up wishing you had Larry as a back-up."

"No chance," Riley said. "There's no way I ever want to have a date with Larry again – for studying or anything else."

Riley heard a noise behind her. She turned to see what it was.

Larry was standing right behind her in her doorway!

chapter
eight

"Sierra, I've got to go," Riley said. "Larry's here."

"Oops!" Sierra said.

"Yeah, talk to you later." Riley hung up the phone. "So…Larry…what's up?"

"Hi." Larry grinned.

"Um, how long have you been standing there?" Riley asked.

"I just got here," Larry said. "I came over to give you this." He handed her a small wire cage. "So you'll have a place to put the missing frog, if you find him."

Phew. He didn't hear me say I never wanted to go out with him again! Riley thought. That would have been harsh.

"Thanks," Riley said. "I think there's a frog in my bathroom."

Larry walked towards the bathroom and peeked inside. "I see it," he said softly.

He calmly bent down and captured the little frog.

Why can't he be normal like this all the time? Riley wondered.

Larry carefully slid the frog into his pocket. "I'll still leave the cage for you," he said, "in case there are more."

"Thanks," Riley said.

"And I brought you a chocolate croissant," Larry added. "I know they're your favourite."

"Really?" Riley's face lit up. She adored chocolate croissants. "Where is it?"

"Downstairs on the kitchen counter," Larry said.

He's being so sweet, Riley thought, feeling like a total jerk.

"Anyway, I've got to go. Sorry to interrupt your phone call," Larry said.

"That's okay," Riley answered. "You didn't hear anything, did you? It was, um, kind of a secret."

"Nope," Larry said. "Scout's honour." He shot her one of his lovesick smiles.

"Okay. See you tomorrow," Riley called as Larry turned and went back down the stairs.

Wow, she thought, when he was gone. He can be so nice sometimes. But then there were the other times...

And no matter what Sierra said, Riley knew how she really felt about Larry. He just wasn't right for her. Period.

"Do you realise the party is only two days away, and neither of us has a date?" Chloe moaned as she walked with Riley towards the lunchroom the next day. "Not that we *have* to have dates. But that was the whole plan."

"I know," Riley agreed, feeling a little panicked. "We can't let this go on any longer."

Rebecca walked towards them in the hall. She darted over, holding her hair up in a ponytail with her hands. "Lost my scrunchie. Anyway, I wanted to ask you: is it dressy or casual?" she said.

"The party? Dressy," Chloe answered.

"Casual," Riley said at the same time.

"Make that dressy-casual," Riley decided.

"In other words, just wear whatever we want?" Rebecca asked, dashing off without waiting for an answer.

"Everyone's so totally ready for this party except us," Riley said.

"I know. I invited Carrie, and she's bringing John. Half the people I know are coming with dates," Chloe said.

"Wow," Riley said.

"So today is our absolute deadline," Chloe announced. "Either we get dates by four o'clock this afternoon or we'll be practically the only ones going solo to our own party. Not a good thing."

"Make that five o'clock," Riley corrected her. "I won't see Alex until after school, at Sierra's band practise."

"Oh, right. And I won't get a chance to talk to Travis until detention either. Okay — five o'clock," Chloe agreed.

"How's your detention plan coming along, anyway?" Riley asked.

"Yesterday was a flop, but I'm on it," Chloe said. "Don't worry. See you later."

"Hey – there he is now!" Riley said, nudging her sister in the ribs.

"Who? Where?" Chloe asked.

"There!" Riley nodded towards the end of the hall. Travis was coming right towards them. "Why don't you invite him now?"

"Just like that?" Chloe asked nervously. "You mean, without getting detention first? Without levelling the playing field? Without getting a rap sheet of my own so he'll know I'm his type of woman? Without…"

"Never mind," Riley said. "He's gone."

"So I'll see him in detention," Chloe said cheerfully, sighing with relief. "Wish me luck!"

Riley laughed as she watched her sister race up the stairs to her next class. Then she walked into the cafeteria and scanned the room, hoping to see Alex. Finally she spotted him, sitting alone in a corner, writing in that black notebook of his.

I wonder what he's writing all the time, she thought.

She was trying to get up the nerve to go over and say hi when she spotted Larry waving to her frantically.

Okay, at least I can be nice to him, she decided. She walked towards his table to see what he wanted.

"Riley! I bought lunch for us," he announced. "I

made sure that I got all of your favourite things to eat!"

Riley stared at the cafeteria tray on the table. It was piled high with every single food available from the kitchen. Salads, sandwiches, the hot meal, tacos, veggie wraps, desserts, milk, juice, yogurt, fruit – it was enough food for a whole baseball team!

"Larry, what is this?" she asked.

"I thought we'd eat together, now that we're going out," he said.

"Larry, we are *not* going out," Riley replied. "We had one study date. That's all."

"I know," Larry admitted. "But you have to eat lunch, don't you? I wasn't sure what you wanted, so I got one of everything. I figured your favourite stuff has to be here somewhere."

Riley sighed. If another guy had done that, it might have seemed romantic or cute. With Larry, it was just plain annoying.

Still, she hated to hurt his feelings. And she *was* hungry. And maybe Sierra was right. Maybe he'd act more normal when he calmed down.

"Okay, but sit down," Riley said. "Everyone's staring at us."

She glanced at the tray of food, trying to figure out what to eat. Finally she picked up a tuna sandwich and took a bite.

"So, can we have another study date this afternoon?" Larry asked.

"Sorry, I can't," Riley said firmly. "I'm going to Sierra's band practise. And Larry?"

"Yes?" He sounded so eager to please.

"Please don't follow me this time, okay?" she said nicely.

Larry started to answer as Mr. Rigsby, a maths teacher, walked by. He was the most unpopular teacher in the whole school.

"Ugh," Larry muttered. "I can't stand Mr. Rigsby."

"How come?" Riley asked.

"I don't know what his problem is," Larry answered. "He's always telling me to stop chewing gum, even when I'm not chewing anything."

"I don't like him either," Riley admitted. "He's so unfair to everyone."

"You want to see something?" Larry said. He sucked some apple juice into his straw, then lifted the straw up and aimed it at the teacher.

"Don't!" Riley said, trying to stop him.

At the sound of her voice, Larry turned in Riley's direction. Unfortunately, he had already begun to blow the juice out of the straw. A stream of it shot out, drenching her face.

"Aaaphh!" Riley cried.

"Sorry!" Larry jumped up and grabbed some napkins. He hurried to her side of the table to wipe off her face.

"Larry! Stop!" Riley yelled, trying to get away from him as he leaned over her, wiping at her forehead.

"Sorry! It was an accident!" Larry explained over and over.

He sounded so sincere, Riley couldn't act as angry as she felt. She let him wipe off the juice with the napkins, mainly so he'd stop apologising.

"Okay. That's good," Riley said, trying to be nice.

"Sorry," Larry said again, dabbing at the tip of her nose. "Hey – you smell kind of good. Like apples or something."

Riley laughed. "That's because you squirted me with *apple* juice," she said. "What do you expect?"

Suddenly she spotted someone out of the corner of her eye. Someone walking by very slowly. Someone watching them as Larry made a final dab on her nose.

Alex.

Their eyes met.

Oh, no! Riley thought. Now he *really* thinks Larry and I are going out! Riley jumped up and started to follow him, to explain it all. "Alex?" she called, practically chasing after him.

I know he heard me. He had to have heard me.

But he didn't stop or turn around. He just hurried down the hall and disappeared.

chapter
nine

"There she is," Chloe announced to Amanda. She leaned against a row of lockers.

"Who?" Amanda asked, staring down the hall.

"Rosalie," Chloe explained. "A total troublemaker. She used to take my lunch money at least once a week in seventh grade. I've got to talk to her."

"I'm thinking she's already spent the money," Amanda joked.

"Ha, ha," Chloe said. "No, really. I'm going to get her to help me with Travis."

Amanda blinked. "I don't get it. How can she help? You mean because he's a real bad boy? Kind of her type?"

"No, no, no," Chloe said. "He's not like her at all. But I figure she can help me get detention. I'll be right back."

Chloe hitched her backpack over her shoulder and slowly made her way towards Rosalie, through the crowds of kids in the hall.

Rosalie was surrounded by her posse – a group of five girls and one punky little guy. All of them were dressed in black denim, and most of them had multiple piercings. It made Chloe's teeth hurt just to look at one girl's lip.

Rosalie herself stood out from the others, partly because her hair was dyed four different colours, in four different clumps – red, orange, purple, and blue – and partly because she was bigger than everyone else.

"Excuse me," Chloe said, trying to muscle her way into the group. "Can I talk to you?"

Rosalie eyed her suspiciously. "What."

It was more of a challenge than a question.

"I need some advice," Chloe said.

"Less lip gloss," Rosalie replied, and her friends all laughed.

"Give me a break," Chloe said. "I really want to ask you something. Can we talk privately?"

Rosalie shrugged and nodded towards a quieter corner. "What's the problem?" she asked, sounding almost interested to hear what Chloe had to say.

"I'm trying to get detention," Chloe explained.

Rosalie tilted her head, sizing up Chloe. "I'm trying to figure out what could possibly make someone like *you* want to get detention. I'm thinking it's a guy."

"Yeah," Chloe admitted.

"Thought so," Rosalie said.

"But I'm sort of...not cut out for it," Chloe went on. "I mean, I have a hard time getting into trouble."

"I feel so sorry for you," Rosalie said sarcastically.

"Well, can you give me some ideas? I mean, what works for you?" Chloe asked.

Rosalie laughed. "I don't actually go around trying to get detention," she said. "But if I did, I'd stick to what I did in middle school – taking lunch money from kids. Conner was the principal at my school in sixth grade, and it drove him nuts. I bet it still will."

"Excellent!" Chloe said, getting into it. "But I can't just go up to someone and take his lunch money. I wouldn't know what to say."

"It's easy," Rosalie said. "Watch and learn." She scanned the crowd and picked out two very small, geeky-looking freshmen guys. Then she motioned for her posse to back her up.

"Hey, dudes," Rosalie said, backing the two guys against a wall. "You owe me for that paper I loaned you last week. Remember?"

The smaller of the two guys looked nervous. "What paper?" he asked.

"The paper," Rosalie said firmly. "That I loaned you. In class."

She sounds really ticked off, Chloe thought. And she's just making this all up as she goes along!

"You're not even in any of my classes," the guy protested, his voice rising in fear.

"Well, I'm *going* to be if you don't pay me back for that paper!" she snapped.

This is amazing, Chloe thought. She watched Rosalie with a mixture of fear, admiration, and respect. If it weren't so wrong, I'd be really impressed. She's so good at what she does!

Suddenly Chloe sensed someone standing behind them. She whirled around and saw Mr. Connor towering over them. He clamped a meaty hand on Rosalie's shoulder and spun her around.

"Up to your old tricks, Miss Puglia?" he asked. "Shaking down students for lunch money?"

"No, wait!" Chloe said. "It was my idea!"

"Don't be ridiculous, Chloe," he said. "Rosalie, I want you in my office for the rest of the lunch period. And you've got detention after school."

Rosalie shot Chloe a glare. A really angry glare.

"You'd better get her out of that," one of Rosalie's friends said.

"But I tried!" Chloe protested. "I tried to tell Mr. Conner the truth, and he wouldn't believe me!"

"Try harder," another girl added. Then they marched away.

Chloe slinked back to where Amanda was waiting.

"Well, that went well," Amanda said.

"Yeah, getting into trouble isn't as easy as it looks," Chloe said. "I'm going to have to throw myself into this full time."

"I don't know," Amanda said. "It seems to me you're getting in plenty of trouble...but with the wrong people."

"Well, I started this, and I'm going to finish it," Chloe said, marching down the hall.

"Where are you going?" Amanda asked.

"To toilet-paper the girls' bathroom," Chloe replied. "I'm on a mission, here. I've got to get detention by the end of the day!"

[Chloe: I admit that deep in my heart I knew this plan wasn't going to work. I mean, I'm too much of a clean freak to really do a job on the girls' bathroom. I pulled some toilet paper off the roll and started flinging it around, but it just looked way too messy that way. So I started draping it carefully across the tops of the stalls. More like decorating. By the time I was done, the bathroom looked like it was all decked out in crepe paper for a birthday party. Then the paper started falling on Jessica Chang. She got annoyed and pulled it all down – just as Mrs. Remmington walked in. Oops! Now Jessica will be spending time in detention this afternoon with Travis – and I won't. Talk about delinquency-challenged! But I'm not giving up. Not yet.]

"Chloe, what are you doing?" Amanda asked later that day.

Chloe was standing on the library table.

"Unscrewing the light bulbs," Chloe answered. "You get detention for a total blackout, don't you?"

"I guess," Amanda answered. "I don't know anyone who's tried it."

"Hey!" someone said in a loud whisper from a table behind them. "Cut it out. I can't see."

Chloe looked over her shoulder and saw Alex sitting there. He was still writing in that black notebook of his.

I wonder what he's writing all the time? she thought. Riley would really like to know.

"Sorry, but we need a blackout in here," Chloe told him. She climbed down without screwing the light bulb back in.

Alex frowned and stood up. He hopped up on to the table and reached for the bulb. "No way," he said. "I need light."

"What's this? Another prank?" Mr. Conner's voice boomed from the library door.

Chloe turned and saw him watching them.

Good! I'm finally going to get detention!

"Alex, you know better than that," Mr. Conner said. "I'm surprised at you. I'll see you in detention after school, buddy."

"No, wait!" Chloe cried. "It's not his fault! It's mine! I did it. Really!"

The vice principal shook his head and gave her a tolerant smile. "Chloe, I'm sure you've got a good reason for standing up for all these troublemakers," he said. "But whatever you're thinking, it's off base. You're wasting your time with most of them."

"No, honestly," Chloe begged him. "Don't give Alex detention – give it to me. I unscrewed all the light bulbs. Why won't you believe me?"

"Chloe, I'm finding this a little annoying," Mr. Conner said. He motioned his head towards the door. "Alex, you can start serving your detention right now. The bell will ring in a few minutes anyway."

Chloe covered her eyes in frustration. "Riley's going to kill me," she whispered to Amanda.

"How come?" Amanda asked.

"She was all psyched to talk to Alex after school at his band rehearsal. Now he won't be able to go," Chloe whispered.

"Uh-oh," Amanda said.

"Yeah," Chloe moaned, uncovering her eyes. "What am I going to do?"

"Apologise, I guess," Amanda said with a shrug.

Chloe nodded. "Right. But what about Travis? What about detention? What about the party? I mean, I'm desperate here. I've got to do something!"

Amanda thought for a minute. "Well, there's still one surefire way to get detention," she said.

"What?" Chloe asked.

"Cut school," Amanda said matter-of-factly.

Hmm. Cut school? Me? West Malibu's Good Citizen of the Month?

"Excellent! I'll do it," Chloe announced. "And tomorrow I'll get detention for sure!"

chapter
ten

"A double skim mocha latte," Riley told the guy behind the counter at California Dream. "I need something to cheer me up."

"Hitting the caffeine hard, are we?" Sierra asked with a laugh.

Riley took a sip of her double mocha and nodded. They sat down in a booth with a view of the beach.

"It was either this or a two-pizza dinner, " Riley confessed. "I'm drowning my sorrows about Alex."

"You're *that* upset – just because we had to cancel band practice?" Sierra sounded surprised.

Riley nodded again. "Definitely. I mean, how can I ask him to the party if I never get a chance to talk to him?"

"And I hear it's all *your* fault that he has detention," Sierra said to Chloe, who had just arrived.

"What's wrong with me?" Chloe said. "I can't get in trouble no matter how hard I try."

"No, but you've got half the kids in school in trouble instead," Riley said in a grumpy voice. "Including the guy I'm supposed to be spending the afternoon with."

"Sorry," Chloe said sheepishly. "At least I come bearing news. I was hanging around outside the detention room after school, hoping to run into Travis..."

"And?" Riley asked.

"I missed Travis," Chloe reported. "Because I had to hide when Rosalie and her friends walked by. But I *did* see Alex. He didn't seem too angry or anything. I mean, he wasn't complaining about me like the other kids were. He was writing in that notebook he's always carrying around."

"What could he possibly be writing that takes all day?" Riley wondered out loud.

"A long love-note to another girl?" Sierra teased Riley.

"Don't tell me that," Riley complained.

Sierra laughed. "Look, chill, okay? You've still got tomorrow to ask him to the party."

"Tomorrow? Tomorrow's Thursday!" Chloe cried. "The party is Friday. This is an emergency. We need dates!"

"Well, Riley, if all else fails, you've still got Larry," Sierra joked.

"Oh, now you're just trying to torment me," Riley

complained.

"Look," Sierra said. Her face was serious. "If you want Alex at the party, why don't you just ask our band to play?"

Riley's eyes lit up. She and Chloe exchanged glances. Yes! That was an excellent plan! Why hadn't they thought of it themselves? Sierra's band was so cool. It would really make the party special.

"Can you?" Riley asked. "On such short notice?"

"Def," Sierra said. "Not a problem."

Great! Riley thought. Except Alex would be busy playing music all night. He wouldn't be her date.

What fun would that be?

"We can put the band on the deck," Chloe suggested. "Unless it rains."

"It never rains in Malibu," Sierra reminded her.

"Then we're all set," Chloe said.

"How many people are coming?" Sierra asked. "I need to figure out how many speakers and amps to bring."

"Who knows?" Chloe answered. "I invited ten people, and Rebecca alone told half the school about the party."

Riley took another drink from her double mocha. It wasn't helping. She didn't feel the least bit cheered up.

Okay, so Alex would be at the party. But that didn't guarantee anything. It didn't mean that he'd even talk to her when the band took breaks.

It's because Alex thought she was seeing Larry.

[**Riley**: **If this wasn't happening to me, I'd kind of think it was funny. I mean, who would have ever imagined that a guy I really liked would be jealous of my relationship with Larry. It's amazing.**]

"Can you tell Alex that Larry and I are just friends?" Riley said, suddenly blurting out what she'd been thinking about.

Sierra glanced towards the door. "You can tell him yourself," she said softly. "Here he comes."

Riley stared across the mostly-empty restaurant. There was Alex, wearing the most perfect retro T-shirt and black jeans Riley had ever seen.

He's walking straight towards me! He's going to talk to me! Riley thought.

Correction: *hoped*.

But he wasn't making eye contact with her at all.

"Sierra," Alex said, "what's up? I thought we had rehearsal."

"I thought you had detention," she said.

"I did, but Conner let us out early," Alex replied. "You want to play some music? We've still got time."

"We can't," Sierra said. "I mean, Saul and Josh went to check out motor scooters. And Marta is…who knows where? Nobody wanted to rehearse without you, so they all split."

"Man," Alex said, scowling.

Riley nudged her sister. "Apologise," she whispered.

Chloe gulped. "Alex, um, I'm really sorry about what happened in the library this afternoon," she said.

Alex nodded, but he still seemed bummed. He headed for a video game machine in the corner and dropped a few quarters in.

Wow, Riley thought. He won't even look at Chloe, either.

"Go talk to him," Sierra said under her breath.

"Okay," Riley said. She forced herself to stand.

It's now or never, she told herself. She crossed the room towards Alex. What should I say? I guess I'll just start with hi, she decided, then see where it goes from there.

Just then, the door swung open and Larry burst in. "Riley!" he shouted, flinging his arms open wide and calling her name as if she were the most perfect human being on the planet.

He started towards her, but a chair leg got in his way. All at once, Larry was tripping, flailing, falling forwards... and Riley was catching him.

"Ow! Larry!" she tried to say. But with his tall, lanky frame leaning on her, it just came out like a muffled cry.

Larry laughed happily. "I fall, and you're there to catch me!" he said, sounding like a lovesick fool. He let his whole body go limp so that Riley would have to hold him up.

Don't! Riley wanted to say. Get off me!

But she couldn't say anything because her eyes were locked on Alex. For a moment, he had turned away from his video game and was watching them. And Riley knew in an instant what he was thinking.

He thinks we're hugging. He thinks I *like* this.

No, you don't understand! Riley wanted to shout. He tripped and fell. It was a total accident!

But before she could explain it, Alex walked out of California Dream without even finishing his game.

"Wait…don't leave," Riley said.

Too late. He was gone.

"Oh, boy. I am so sorry," Larry started apologising.

"That's okay," Riley muttered, feeling miserable.

What am I going to do? she wondered. I know Larry isn't doing it on purpose, but he's ruining my love life!

"Can I get you something?" Larry asked, following her like a puppy dog.

"No!" Riley snapped. "Just leave me alone!"

Larry's face fell. Riley had never yelled at him like that before. "Sorry," he said, backing away. Then he left.

Riley instantly felt horrible. She'd have to call Larry tonight to apologise. "Let's go," she said to her sister. "I've got homework. And we'd better tell Mom that we're going to have a band at the party."

"Okay." Chloe stood up, but she didn't look any happier than Riley felt.

"Hey, don't worry, you guys," Sierra said. "Whatever happens, at least you'll have an awesome party to forget your troubles. It's going to be a blast. You'll see."

Right, Riley thought. For everyone except us. How did things get so messed up? "Can you talk to Alex?" she whispered to Sierra. "Could you tell him I'm not going out with Larry?"

Sierra nodded. "I'll see what I can do."

"Thanks," Riley said, and she and Chloe headed out.

When the girls got home, Manuelo had his special pasta and shrimp dish in the oven. The house smelled wonderful, of garlic, oregano, and cheese.

"What's wrong with you two?" he asked, frowning and putting his hands on his hips. "You look like the little kittens who have lost their mittens."

"We're just a little down about the party," Chloe said.

"Oh, how can you be down about a party?" Manuelo asked. "Look at all the candles I bought to make the house look fabulous."

He gestured towards an awesome collection of rose, orange, and rust-coloured candles in all sizes and shapes. Riley liked the ones with white flowers embedded in the middle best.

"They're great, Manuelo," Riley said. "Thanks."

"And look in the living room," he went on. "I've moved the furniture so there's a better traffic flow to the food."

"Good idea," Chloe said, cheering up a little. "Now all we have to do is figure out where to put the band."

"Band? I didn't know we were having a band," Manuelo said, frowning.

"Oh, yeah, we definitely are," Riley said. "My friend Sierra's band is going to play."

"We were thinking out on the deck," Chloe chimed in. "But the neighbours might complain if it's too loud."

Manuelo shook his head doubtfully. "I'll have to talk to your mother about it. I'm not sure that's what she had in mind."

"I'm sure she'll agree to the band," Riley said. "Good music is the key to a good party."

"Where is she?" Chloe asked anxiously.

"She's out having a business dinner with a client," Manuelo replied. "She might be late, too."

It'll work out, Riley thought as she gazed around the room. Manuelo was really doing an amazing job. The house is going to look great. And the party is going to be awesome… I just hope Sierra gets a chance to talk to Alex.

chapter
eleven

"Are you sure you want to cut class with me?" Chloe asked Amanda the next morning at school.

Today was the day. Chloe was going to get detention no matter what it took.

Amanda shrugged. "Why not?" she said. "It'll be fun. Besides, my French teacher is out today, so I'm not missing anything. The only thing is, I've got to be back in time for a test in algebra."

"Okay, great," Chloe said. "We'll be mall rats from second period till fifth."

"But remember, I don't want to get detention," Amanda said. "So I'm sneaking in a side door when we get back."

"Not a problem," Chloe said. "You can sneak in while I'm making myself obvious enough to get caught."

Chloe's eyes sparkled and Amanda laughed. "I've never seen anyone so happy about the idea of getting detention in my whole, entire life," Amanda declared.

"I'm desperate," Chloe admitted. "I've got to talk to Travis, and detention is the only chance I have."

"Hey, do you think he'll notice that we're absent from the lunchroom?" Amanda wondered.

"I hope so!" Chloe cried.

[**Chloe**: "Where were you in lunch today? I missed you," Travis says as I waltz into the detention room with a proudly defiant look on my face.

"I couldn't take it any more," I answer. "I had to get away. I can't bear being around you, being so close to you every day in school, and not being allowed to be alone together."

"Don't do that again," Travis says, brushing my cheek with his hand. "Don't cut lunch. It's just not the same when you're not there..."

Hey, a girl can dream, can't she?]

"Chloe? Hey, Chloe!" Amanda snapped her fingers.

"Huh?" Chloe said.

"Where were you?" Amanda asked.

"Never mind," Chloe answered. "Let's go."

The two of them slipped out of the building, caught a bus, and were at the mall in twenty minutes.

Inside, Chloe felt a mixture of giddy excitement and guilt. "I hope we don't get caught!" she said.

"I thought getting caught was the whole point," Amanda said.

"Yes, but caught by Mr. Conner," Chloe explained. "Not by my parents."

"Is that a possibility?" Amanda looked freaked.

"I don't know. I've never done this before," Chloe confessed. "It feels really weird to be in the mall in the middle of a school day."

"I know," Amanda agreed. "I cut school once, in the fifth grade, but I was scared to death. I sneaked out of art class to go to this little grocery store a block away. Blew my whole lunch money on Hostess cupcakes."

Chloe laughed and linked arms with Amanda. "Ooh, check out those jeans!" she said, steering them towards Lala's, a hip new clothing store.

She ploughed through the racks of jeans quickly and grabbed a pair of cords in burgundy. They looked fabulous with an orange lacy crocheted sweater. She also picked out a short little dress for Amanda and two pairs of leather jeans, just for fun.

She thrust the clothes at Amanda. "Try these on."

"Really?" Amanda hesitated.

"Oh, they'll be so perfect for you!" Chloe insisted. "That sweater goes great with your hair. I remember seeing something like it in that fashion magazine. And if it fits, you could wear it to the party tomorrow night."

Chloe sat on the bench in the dressing room with her feet up and her arms wrapped around her knees. Amanda tossed off her blue jeans and black stretch T-shirt, and pulled the orange sweater over her head.

so little time

I wonder why she always wears jeans, Chloe thought. Then she noticed that Amanda wasn't wearing the lip gloss that Chloe had given her.

Amanda turned to show Chloe the sweater.

"It looks amazing," Chloe said. "It even brings out your freckles."

"I don't know," Amanda said, laughing again. "I'm not sure if I'm the orange type."

"Oh, but you are," Chloe said, jumping up. "And where's the lip gloss I gave you? It's a great colour with that outfit."

"I'm not sure," Amanda said. "I think it's in my bag."

"You've got to put it on!" Chloe urged her.

Amanda looked uncomfortable, but she reached into her backpack and fished out the lip gloss. She swished some on to her lips.

I was right, Chloe thought. It looks perfect!

"I think you should buy that outfit," Chloe declared. "It's so fabulous on you. Here, let me put your hair up, the way I did the other day."

She started to pull Amanda's hair back and separate it into sections. But Amanda turned to face her. "You know what? I don't really want to change my hair," she said, looking Chloe directly in the eye. "And this outfit is nice, you're right. But it's really not my style. I like myself the way I am. Why do you keep pushing me to change?"

"Oh." Chloe instantly felt horrible. "Sorry," she said. "I didn't mean to push you. Why didn't you tell me before that you didn't like the stuff that I picked out?"

Amanda shrugged. "It's fun to try new things," she said. "And I didn't want to hurt your feelings. But no offence, I like my own style. For me, I mean."

Wow, Chloe thought. Most of the girls Chloe knew cared more about each other's opinions than that. But Amanda seemed so sure of herself. So much more confident than Chloe had realised. She didn't need anyone else's approval. That's so...great!

"I'm really sorry, Amanda," Chloe said. "I guess I got carried away. Put me in a clothing store and I'll start making over the mannequins!"

"That's not a bad idea." Amanda laughed. "Since the ones in Lala's window don't have any heads!"

Chloe glanced at her watch. They still had plenty of time before they needed to be back at school. She tried on two skirts, four tops, two pairs of jeans, and a hat. But none of them were all that great.

"I'm starved," Amanda said. "Shopping definitely burns more calories than history class."

"Me, too," Chloe agreed, leaving the store empty-handed.

They grabbed a quick lunch in the food court. After that, Amanda bought a new pair of hiking boots. Then they headed back to school.

"I'll meet you by your locker," Chloe said as she left Amanda by the side door. "I'm going in through the front. I want to make sure I get caught."

"You got it," Amanda said. She switched her shopping bag to her left hand and pulled open the door.

Chloe circled the school. She skipped happily up the steps to the main door and entered. Hmm, she wondered, should I bother giving the security guard an excuse? To make it seem more believable?

But none of that mattered. The security guard wasn't at the front door. "Hey!" Chloe yelled. "Anybody home?"

Chloe's shoulders slumped. How could this be happening? There was always a security guard posted by the front door. Why not today?

She sighed and decided to head towards Amanda's locker. She passed through the main hallway, when she noticed a little commotion by the side door.

"Uh-oh," she muttered when she saw what was happening. She had found the security guard. He was with Mr. Conner – and Amanda.

Mr. Conner was standing with his hands on his hips. His famous 'caught-another-one' sneer was creeping on to his face.

"I know you were cutting school, Amanda," he said. "I don't want to hear your excuses."

"B-but, I— " Amanda stammered.

"No excuses," Mr. Conner repeated. "I want to see you in my office. And you've got detention for the rest of the week!"

chapter
twelve

"**S**top!" Chloe rushed up to Mr. Conner. "Don't give her detention. It's *my* fault. We went to the mall. I'm the one who wanted to cut school!"

Mr. Conner shot Chloe a sideways glance. "You know what, Chloe?" he said, with just the slightest bit of irritation in his voice. "I'm really beginning to get tired of this. You can't keep trying to take the blame for other people's mistakes. They'll never learn that way."

"No, please," Chloe pleaded. "Honestly, I was cutting school. It was all my idea. I'*m* the shopaholic here – not Amanda. Can't you tell? Just look at me!" Chloe twirled around to model the checked bell-bottom jeans and stretchy little pink top she was wearing.

Mr. Conner pointed to the security guard. "Look, Chloe. Hal caught her sneaking into school with that."

Hal held up Amanda's shopping bag. "There's no way you can get your friend out of this one."

Chloe couldn't think of a reply. The bell rang.

"Amanda – my office, right now," Mr. Conner said. "Chloe, please go on to class."

"Mr. Conner, I have an algebra test this period," Amanda said in a desperate voice.

"Well, you'll be a few minutes late," Mr. Connor said. "You have to see me in my office, first."

By now, the hall was filled with hundreds of students heading to their next class. Chloe saw Travis and Cameron emerge from a classroom.

"Amanda, I'm really sorry," Chloe said.

Amanda shrugged and tried to look like she wasn't upset. "It's okay. I'm sure Mr. Fiorello will let me take a few minutes longer on the test. I just don't want to get a zero."

"Don't worry," Travis said, strolling over to Amanda. "Detention isn't so bad. Just sit in the back so you can eat without being seen. Hang with me. I'll show you."

Chloe tried to catch Travis's attention, but he just smiled at Amanda and they walked away.

Oh, no! Chloe thought, watching him with Amanda. That was supposed to be me!

Chloe rolled out of bed on Friday morning and hit the shower. She felt miserable, but she tried to look on the bright side. At least we're having a party tonight and lots of people are coming.

That was the good news. The bad news, however, was longer:

1. She had slept on her face, and now there was a deep crease in her cheek. It probably wouldn't go away until fifth period.
2. Practically the whole school was avoiding her as if she was some kind of detention jinx. And who could blame them?
3. There was almost no chance that she'd get to talk to Travis and invite him to the party.
4. Riley was just as grumpy as she was.

I'm an idiot, Chloe thought. Why did I spend this whole week trying to get detention anyway? It was a crazy plan. I should have done what Amanda said – just tried to be myself.

She pulled a pair of jeans and a top out of her closet and got dressed, barely bothering to glance in the mirror. Then she stuffed a yogurt in her backpack to eat on the way to school, since she was already running late.

"Wow, are *you* in a bad mood," Quinn said as Chloe dragged herself towards West Malibu High.

"It shows that much?" Chloe asked.

Quinn looked her up and down. "That top? With those shoes? Are you kidding?" she said. "I mean, not that it matters, Chloe, but it's not like you."

Chloe looked down at what she was wearing and gasped. Quinn was right. The red snakeskin pumps didn't exactly go with the grey hooded sweatshirt.

As they neared the front door, Quinn stopped walking and stood still, letting Chloe go on without her.

"What's wrong now?" Chloe said. "You can't stand to be seen with me?"

"I just don't want to get detention," Quinn replied. "Sorry. Can you go in alone?"

Can this get any worse? Chloe wondered.

Another crowd of kids hanging out by the front door scattered when they saw her coming.

Everyone's acting as though I have leprosy or something! Chloe realised. She yanked open the door and stepped into the building, feeling even worse. Trying to get detention was totally ruining her social life.

From now on, it's back to being West Malibu's Good Citizen of the Month, she decided. She pulled her empty yogurt container from her backpack and tossed it towards the trash can.

"Oops! Missed," Chloe said as the yogurt container missed the can and hit the floor.

"Littering, Chloe? That's not like you," a voice said from behind.

Chloe whirled around. Mr. Conner was looming over her. "But I just..." she started to say.

"No excuses," Conner said. "You've been begging for detention all week, so all right. You've got it. See me after school."

"But I didn't do that on purpose," Chloe protested.

"I saw you throw it," Connor replied. "And you didn't even aim for the basket. You just tossed it on the floor."

"I *did* aim," Chloe said. "Come on. Can I help it if I'm

a lousy shot?" She started to argue, but then stopped.

Hold on. This is my big chance to get detention with Travis!

"Okay," Chloe said, smiling. "See you after school!"

For the rest of the day, she was in a fantastic mood. Detention! With Travis! It was what she'd been hoping for all week!

It wasn't too late to invite him to the party, was it?

Plus now she was almost positive he'd say yes. Now that she had something in common with him.

"Riley, I've got detention!" she announced when she ran into her sister in the hall after fifth period.

"No way. That's terrible. We've got a million things to do to get ready for the party tonight," Riley said.

"I'll only be an hour late," Chloe said. "Can you handle it till I get home?"

"I guess," Riley agreed. "Thank goodness Manuelo is so organised. He's got it together."

True, Chloe thought. The party was going to be awesome, thanks to him. Without even being asked, he'd gone ahead and got everything done.

When school was over, she raced to her locker to get the 'emergency' outfit she kept on hand at all times. It was a fabulous black skirt and white top. It even went with the red shoes!

In the bathroom, she twisted her hair into a knot on top of her head. Then she ran all the way to the detention room on the third floor, so she wouldn't be late.

Travis stood in the doorway as she dashed into the classroom.

"Hi, Travis!" Chloe said, beaming at him and almost skidding to a stop.

I didn't even get tongue-tied, she thought. Her heart was racing, partly from running up the steps and partly because he was so unbelievably cute.

"Whoa! Slow down," Travis said, putting out his hands to catch her if she fell.

Okay, so maybe I'm rushing, Chloe thought. But this is perfect! It's as if he was just standing there, waiting for me to talk to him.

"Guess what?" she said, smiling proudly. "I've got detention!"

"Really?" Travis sort of squinted at her as if he didn't believe it. "Not me. I'm out of here."

Huh? Chloe couldn't believe what she was hearing.

"But why?" she asked him. As in, how could you!

"The monitor let me out a day early, for good behaviour," he explained. He shot her a pleased-with-himself smile.

For good behaviour? Chloe couldn't think about that. The main thing was that Travis was about to get away!

"Uh, listen," she said, getting right to the point. "I'm having a party tonight at our house, and, uh, it would be cool if you could come."

Travis broke into a weird smile and shook his head. "I don't think so," he said. "Everyone you hang with gets detention. And I promised my parents I'd stay away from people who could get me into trouble."

No! Chloe thought, her heart sinking. Was he kidding? He didn't want to be around her because *she* was trouble?

Her shoulders slumped as he strolled out of the room. She couldn't believe this. She'd spent the whole week trying to get detention – *for nothing*!

chapter
thirteen

"**W**hat? What's wrong?" Chloe stopped in her tracks and froze the minute she stepped into her house. She could tell immediately from the panicked look on Riley's face that something was terribly wrong.

"Big problem," Riley said, pointing to the kitchen counter. "Look."

Chloe glanced at the array of wine and wine glasses that were set up on the counter. Beside them was a nice arrangement of cocktail napkins and mixed nuts.

Wine?

"Manuelo, what's going on?" Chloe asked. "We can't have wine at our party. Mom will have a fit."

"It's not for your party," Manuelo explained. "It's for your *mother's* party. The one she has been planning for two weeks."

"Are you serious?" Chloe was stunned. "But she can't! We're...we've invited..."

"There's been a small misunderstanding," Manuelo said apologetically.

"When we asked Manuelo about having a party, he thought we were talking about Mom's party," Riley added, talking super-fast. "All that food he told us about? All those candles? It's all for her!"

"No," Chloe said. "This is awful. What are we going to do?"

"Talk to your mother," Manuelo replied, shrugging his shoulders and looking so sorry.

Chloe and Riley raced upstairs and waited anxiously for their mother to get out of the shower.

"Sorry, girls," she said after they'd explained the problem. "This is a big deal I'm having for clients. There's no way you can have twenty or thirty of your friends over at the same time."

"I suppose that means fifty would be out of the question," Chloe grumbled.

"Fifty was *always* out of the question," Macy replied.

"But Mom," Riley pleaded. "We *asked* you."

"I'm really sorry. It was an honest mistake," she said. "You'll have to call everyone and cancel."

"Call everyone?" Riley whispered to her sister. "We don't even know everyone who's coming!"

"We'll think of something, Mom," Chloe said. She pulled her sister towards their room so they could brainstorm in private. "Listen, I don't want to cancel either. It makes us look like such losers if we say we're having a party, and then call it off at the last minute. What if we moved the party to the beach?"

"No good," Riley said. "I don't think Mom would go for it. Our party would make too much noise. Besides, the band can't play without someplace to plug in the amps."

"True," Chloe said. She tried to think of something else just as the phone rang. "Hello?"

"Hi," a guy's voice said on the other end. "This is Travis."

Chloe sat up fast, hoping she wouldn't say anything stupid. "Hi!" she said brightly.

"I was just wondering," Travis said. "What's your address?"

"My address?" Chloe asked.

"Yeah," Travis said. "You're having a party, aren't you?"

"Uh, yeah," Chloe replied.

[Chloe: Look, I couldn't help it, okay? I mean, TRAVIS wanted to come. Besides, the party wasn't technically cancelled, yet.]

"So, what time? And where do you live?" Travis asked.

"Um, here's the thing," she said, thinking fast. "We might be moving the party to someone else's house. Can I call you back?"

"Sure," Travis said. He gave her his phone number and hung up.

Chloe glanced at the clock and grabbed Riley's arms. "We've *got* to think of something," she pleaded with her sister. "This is my big chance!"

"Big chance for what?" a voice asked.

Chloe's turned to see Larry peering in their open first-floor window. He was standing on a ladder.

It's my big chance to be with Travis tonight, Chloe thought. But she wasn't going to tell Larry that. "Um, we've got a problem," Chloe started to say.

"Don't," Riley said, shooting Chloe a warning glare.

"Don't?" Chloe repeated. "But you don't even know what I'm going to say."

Chloe wanted to tell Larry about the party problem. She was sure that if she mentioned it, Larry would offer to have the party at his house. It would be so perfect. Larry lived right next door!

But Riley had a really stern look on her face, so Chloe didn't say anything.

"What kind of problem?" Larry asked.

"Never mind," Riley said firmly. "Why did you come over?"

"Can I come in?" he asked, pressing his nose up against the window screen.

Riley popped the screen out of the window and Larry fell into the room, on to the floor.

"I just wanted to apologise," he said, standing up.

"For what?" Riley asked.

"For all that stuff I did," Larry said. "The frogs, and

97

spitting juice at you, and showing up all the time when you're trying to hang out with other people. Anyway, I'm really sorry," he said. "Is there any way I can make it up to you?"

"Yes!" Chloe blurted out before Riley could stop her. "Can we move our party to your house?"

"Party?" Larry asked. "What party?"

Uh-oh. Riley didn't invite him, Chloe realised. And neither did I. She stared at her shoes, feeling like such a creep. "Um, we were going to have a party tonight...." Chloe began.

"Oh, right!" Larry said. "I forgot. I heard about it at school. I was going to stop by."

Chloe looked up. "You were?" She still felt like a creep, but at least Larry didn't seem to be offended.

"So you're *not* having the party?" Larry asked. "How come?"

Chloe tried not to look at her sister when she answered. "Well, the problem is that we can't actually have it at our house because it turns out our mom is having a party at the same time. Major communication error. So I was thinking..."

"Sure!" Larry jumped in. "That would be cool. Have it at my house. I mean, I'll check with my dad, but I know he'll say yes. And it's perfect. We live right next door."

"No way." Riley shook her head firmly.

Chloe almost choked. What does she mean "no way"?

"Can we talk?" Chloe said, dragging Riley out into the hall. She shut their bedroom door, closing Larry inside. "Have you lost it?" she asked Riley when they were alone.

Riley folded her arms across her chest. "Look, if I let Larry do stuff like that for me, I'm just leading him on," Riley explained. "Don't you see? He's going to start thinking he has a chance with me, when he doesn't. I don't want to use him like that."

"You're not using him," Chloe argued. "He offered to help."

"No, you begged him," Riley pointed out.

"I didn't have to beg. He leaped at the chance!" Chloe replied. "He's like, totally happy now. Didn't you see his face? He just wants to do nice things for you because he's so crazy about you."

"I know. That's the problem," Riley said.

"Oh, come on, Riley. This is the only chance we've got," Chloe pleaded. "Otherwise, we're phoning half the school and telling them not to show up tonight. And that includes Alex."

Chloe could see Riley thinking about that.

"Okay," Riley said finally. "We'll have the party at Larry's."

chapter
fourteen

"This is awesome!" Rebecca yelled, trying to be heard above the music.

"Thanks," Chloe said, although she sort of hated to take credit for it.

The party was rocking, thanks to Manuelo and Larry. Manuelo had raced to the store and bought huge platters of quesadillas, cut-up veggies, dips, and hero sandwiches. Plus tons of stuff to drink.

Larry had pushed all the furniture back in his living room, and Chloe and Riley had helped him decorate the whole house – inside and out – with strings and strings of tiny white lights. They lit up the tree by the front door, laced the deck facing the ocean, and hung paper lanterns around the edges of the living room. The whole place looked magical.

Sierra's band was parked in a corner of the living room and Riley stood leaning in a doorway, watching Alex.

Best of all, Travis had actually shown up. He was wearing a pair of really cool shiny black jeans, with a tight royal blue sweater — sort of a retro disco look. It was fabulous.

"What should I say to him?" Chloe asked Amanda. "I mean, I can't believe he actually came!"

"Why don't you just be yourself and find out if he likes you that way?" Amanda suggested. "I mean, you've tried everything else, right?"

Chloe laughed. "You're right," she said, nodding.

She made her way across the living room, past tons of people, dancing. Travis was standing alone near the food table.

Chloe took a deep breath. "Hey, Travis."

"Hey." He gave her a smile. "Your party rocks."

"Thanks," Chloe said. "I'm glad you came."

"Me, too." He gazed down into her eyes.

"I didn't think you would," she added. "I mean, I thought you promised your parents to stay away from people who could get you into trouble."

Travis laughed, and Chloe noticed for the first time that he had two tiny dimples in his left cheek. "That was a joke," he said, grinning. "You thought I was serious?"

"Oh. Well, yeah, sort of," Chloe said. "I thought, well, it's like…" She started to stammer, so she just stopped talking.

"You're not exactly the type my parents would call a 'bad influence'," Travis said, teasing her. But he was still smiling as though he was happy to be hanging out with her.

Wow, Chloe thought. He sort of *likes* the fact that I'm a model student, or whatever. Opposites really *do* attract!

"You want to dance?" he asked, taking her hand and leading her into the crowd before she could answer.

Chloe started moving to the music and closed her eyes. She was so happy. She wanted this song to go on forever.

Look at them, Riley thought, watching her sister dance with Travis. They look so great together.

Chloe had decided against the shimmery red dress. Instead, she had on a short black dress with a blue beaded necklace that almost matched Travis's sweater.

It's as if they planned it, Riley thought, although she knew that was totally not true.

"Have you seen Kyle?" someone asked, shouting to be heard above the amps.

Riley turned and saw Rebecca's friend, Lauren, standing beside her.

"I think he's in the basement," Riley said.

"Cool party!" Lauren said before pushing her way towards the steps.

Riley started to turn back to watch the band. Alex looked amazing, she thought. Just the way he stood there, you could tell he was the most confident one of the group. Other than Sierra, of course, who was always on, always out there, always giving off a great I'm-on-top-of-the-world vibe.

They were doing a song Sierra had written, called 'Blue Temper'. Marta was spinning some tracks to give it an edgy techno beat. Josh wasn't onstage. Riley guessed they had decided not to let him join the band.

Larry came up to her with an expectant look on his face. "Want to dance?" he asked.

Oh, man, Riley thought. He'd already asked her three times and she'd said, "Later."

I can't put him off all night, she thought. After all, I owe him big. "Okay," Riley said, following Larry into the crowd.

The music blared throughout the house, making it hard to hear a conversation, but the song was great to dance to.

And to Riley's amazement, Larry was an awesome dancer! He's such a free spirit, Riley realised. Nothing embarrasses him, which is a great quality to have on the dance floor.

"That was incredible," Riley said when the song was over. She walked towards the food table to grab something to drink. Larry followed her.

"So why are we quitting so soon?" Larry asked. "You want to dance again?"

Riley gulped some bottled water. Time to level with him, she thought. Give it to him straight. Softly...but the truth.

"No thanks, Larry," she said as nicely as she could. "I mean, I really like you as a friend – but that's all. To tell you the truth, I kind of like Alex."

"Alex?" Larry's face tightened up, but he didn't look angry. Just hurt. "So are you saying there's *no* chance we could ever go out again?"

"I'd say it's one in a million," Riley said, nodding.

"Ah-ha! So that means there *is* a chance!" Larry said, beaming.

He can't be serious, Riley thought. She eyed Larry to see if he was joking. Nope.

"Take my word for it, Larry," Riley said. "I think we have to stick to being just friends."

"Okay," he said. "But you know what? I think you're just not ready for me yet. But you will be – someday."

I doubt it, Riley thought as she walked back to her spot near the band.

But wouldn't it be totally weird if he was right?

The band had been playing for almost an hour, and Riley figured it was time for them to take a break. But instead, Alex stepped up to the microphone to announce the next song.

"This is something I wrote this week," he said, staring down, not looking at anyone in the crowd. "It's called 'Don't You Know'."

He opened up the small black notebook – the one he'd been writing in all week – and propped it up on a stool so he could see the words.

So that's what he'd been writing all those times, Riley realised. A song.

Alex counted it off, strummed the opening chords, and started singing.

"Pass her in the hall...Try to catch her smile...Don't you know you're all...I need for a while?"

The song was beautiful, a slow bittersweet melody with great chords. Everyone in the room stopped dancing, and just listened.

"Make me want to change...Make me want to speak...Tell you how I feel...You're the one I seek...."

"He wrote that for someone," Riley heard Rebecca whispering to Lauren as the song went on.

"How do you know?" Lauren said softly.

"You can just tell, can't you?" Rebecca replied.

Rebecca's right, Riley thought. He did write it for someone. But who?

Just then, Alex lifted his head and searched the crowd. His eyes found hers as he sang the last verse.

"Don't you know it's you, girl? Can't you hear the truth? Don't you know it's you? Can't I offer proof?"

Wow, Riley thought, her heart pumping. Maybe he wrote it for me! She stared at him, totally falling for him even harder than she already had.

Okay, so this night was turning out all right. Better than she ever imagined, in fact.

Riley glanced outside and spotted Chloe and Travis

standing together on Larry's deck. Would they get together? she wondered. Was he the guy for Chloe? Only time would tell.

The sound of applause erupted in the room. The song was over, and Alex was smiling shyly into the crowd.

Could he really like me as much as I like him? Riley thought. Is it possible?

Then Alex's smile fell on Riley. A warm, wonderful sensation washed over her as she smiled back, gazing into his deep brown eyes.

Riley couldn't explain why, but she had a good feeling about this boy. A feeling that she was going to get to know Alex really well. And Riley couldn't wait!

Chloe
and Riley's

SCRAPBOOK

so little time

Check out book 3!

too good to be true

"This ice cream is awesome," Riley said to Alex as they strolled along the beach after school. They'd stopped at an ice cream shop earlier, where Alex bought them each a cone.

"Chocolate Raspberry Ripple. It's great, isn't it? It's one of my favourites," Alex said.

Riley felt the cool sand between her bare toes. She tried to focus on what Alex was saying, but her heart was hammering in her chest. She couldn't remember the last time she felt so nervous – or happy.

"So like I was saying before, my mom is a pediatrician," Alex said. "And my dad's a lawyer, although he used to play guitar when he was in high school. Just like me."

"Do you have any brothers or sisters?" Riley asked him.

"I have a little brother, Zach. He's six. I help take care of him a lot, since my mom and dad have such crazy work schedules," Alex replied.

"I know what that's like," Riley said, nodding. "My

mom is a fashion designer. She and my dad used to run the business together, but now they're separated, so she does it all herself. She's pretty nuts all the time."

"That must be tough," Alex said, "your parents being separated and all."

Riley smiled at him. He was so nice. Nice… and cute.

"It was weird at first," she said after a minute. "But they seem to be getting along better, now that they're not living together. If that makes any sense."

"Sure, that makes sense." Alex smiled and moved closer to her.

The next thing she knew, Alex took her hand and squeezed it.

Riley almost dropped her Chocolate Raspberry Ripple into the sand. First they were on a date, and now Alex was holding her hand. This was so unbelievably awesome!

"Um, your band," Riley squeaked. She tried to get her voice under control. "Your band," she repeated. "Sierra told me you guys are playing at California Dream again this weekend." His fingers felt so warm and wonderful intertwined with hers.

"Yeah," Alex said, taking a bite of his cone. "I'm pretty psyched about that. You're coming, aren't you?" he added eagerly. "Maybe we could hang out after the show."

Riley nodded yes, yes, yes. "I wouldn't miss it."

"Great," Alex said.

A wave rolled in, tickled her feet, then receded. The sun glittered on the blue water. Everything was so perfect: the sun… the waves… the palm trees swaying in the breeze… Alex. Riley didn't want their date to ever end.

The beach was deserted. Except for one lone girl jogging toward them. As she neared, Riley noticed that the girl was tall and slender, with a long platinum-blonde ponytail.

Alex noticed her, too – and suddenly dropped Riley's hand.

"Alex!" the girl cried out. She jogged up to him and gave him a big, sweaty hug.

[Riley: Okay, who is this person? Why is she hugging Alex? Why is he hugging her? Why don't they stop hugging, already?]

After what seemed to be hours, the girl untangled her sweaty, perfect body from Alex and beamed at him. "How are you? It's been ages." She squeezed his arm.

"Um, yeah," Alex said. He sounded flustered.

He turned to Riley. "Willow, this is Riley Carlson. Riley, this is Willow Sweet. She's…an old friend of mine."

[Riley: "Old friend?" Do old friends hug like that? I don't think so.]

Willow smiled at Riley. "Hey, it's so nice to meet you! Do you go to West Malibu High, too?"

"Uh-huh," Riley replied. She couldn't stop staring at Willow. She'd never seen anyone so totally pretty before. She was even more gorgeous than Tedi.

"And where do you go to school?" Riley managed to ask after a minute. Say you're visiting from somewhere else, she prayed. Like Australia.

"My family just moved back to Malibu," Willow explained. "We moved away for a while...but now we're back." She reached out and squeezed Alex's arm again.

"You're going to West Malibu High?" Alex asked her, surprised.

Riley noticed that Willow still had her hand on Alex's arm – and that Alex wasn't moving it away. She frowned.

Willow nodded. "Isn't that great? I start classes tomorrow."

Willow said something else to Alex – something about her parents – but Riley barely heard her. Her mind was racing.

Willow seemed super-nice. She also seemed super touchy-feely with Alex. Was it Riley's imagination, or were the two of them definitely more than just "old friends"?

"Riley?"

Riley's head shot up. Alex was staring at her.

"Huh?" Riley said.

"Willow was wondering if you and I could give her

some advice about teachers," Alex said. "Like that sewing teacher – don't you have her? Plus some of the other ones."

"Sure, any time," Riley said to Willow.

"Great! That is so sweet of you. Well, better get back to my jog. See you guys later!" Willow gave a little wave and began running up the beach again.

Riley and Alex resumed their walk. Riley suddenly realised that her ice cream had melted. Her cone was now a sorry-looking, soggy lump – kind of like how she felt inside.

Alex didn't say a word. He didn't take her hand again, either. He just stared ahead at the horizon.

"Soooo," Riley said after a moment. "Willow seems nice."

"Yeah." Alex turned to her abruptly. "Look, I should tell you."

Riley's heart lurched in her chest. "Tell me what?"

"Willow and I used to go out," Alex confessed. "But it was over a long time ago. I just want you to know that."

"Oh, don't worry about it," Riley said, forcing herself to smile. "I totally understand. It's not a problem."

But inside she was thinking, Willow looks like Gwyneth Paltrow. She's even nice. Why was Alex crazy enough to stop dating her? And what's going to stop him from taking up where he left off?

To be continued...

mary-kateandashley

Meet Chloe and Riley Carlson.

So much to do...

so little time

(1)	How to Train a Boy	(0 00 714458 X)
(2)	Instant Boyfriend	(0 00 714448 2)
(3)	Too Good to be True	(0 00 714449 0)
(4)	Just Between Us	(0 00 714450 4)
(5)	Tell Me About It	(0 00 714451 2)
(6)	Secret Crush	(0 00 714452 0)

... and more to come!

HarperCollins*Entertainment*

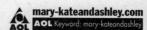

mary-kateandashley

TWO of a kind ™

Coming soon – can you collect them all?

(1)	It's a Twin Thing	(0 00 714480 6)
(2)	How to Flunk Your First Date	(0 00 714479 2)
(3)	The Sleepover Secret	(0 00 714478 4)
(4)	One Twin Too Many	(0 00 714477 6)
(5)	To Snoop or Not to Snoop	(0 00 714476 8)
(6)	My Sister the Supermodel	(0 00 714475 X)
(7)	Two's a Crowd	(0 00 714474 1)
(8)	Let's Party	(0 00 714473 3)
(9)	Calling All Boys	(0 00 714472 5)
(10)	Winner Take All	(0 00 714471 7)
(11)	PS Wish You Were Here	(0 00 714470 9)
(12)	The Cool Club	(0 00 714469 5)
(13)	War of the Wardrobes	(0 00 714468 7)
(14)	Bye-Bye Boyfriend	(0 00 714467 9)
(15)	It's Snow Problem	(0 00 714466 0)
(16)	Likes Me, Likes Me Not	(0 00 714465 2)
(17)	Shore Thing	(0 00 714464 4)
(18)	Two for the Road	(0 00 714463 6)

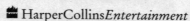
HarperCollins*Entertainment*

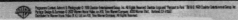

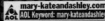

Order Form

To order direct from the publishers, just make a list of the titles you want and fill in the form below:

Name ....

Address ....

....

....

Send to: Dept 6, HarperCollins Publishers Ltd, Westerhill Road, Bishopbriggs, Glasgow G64 2QT.

Please enclose a cheque or postal order to the value of the cover price, plus:

UK & BFPO: Add £1.00 for the first book, and 25p per copy for each additional book ordered.

Overseas and Eire: Add £2.95 service charge. Books will be sent by surface mail but quotes for airmail despatch will be given on request.

A 24-hour telephone ordering service is available to holders of Visa, MasterCard, Amex or Switch cards on 0141- 772 2281.

Collins
An *Imprint of* HarperCollins*Publishers*